HEAD ROCK HARBOR MYSTERY #2

MURDER IN THE ROUGH

CHASE CONNOR

Book Cover Designed By: Chase Connor
©2024 Chase Connor; Chase Connor Books

Published By:

Chase Connor Books
www.chaseconnor.com

AUTHORS' NOTE:
This is a work of fiction. Names, characters, places, and incidents either are the product of the authors' imagination or are used fictitiously, and any resemblance to actual persons, living or dead, business establishments, events, or locales is entirely coincidental. None of this is real.

E-book ISBN 978-1-951860-49-3
Paperback ISBN 978-1-951860-50-9

Also by Chase Connor

LGBTQ+ YA Books

Just a Dumb Surfer Dude: A Gay Coming-of-Age Tale
Just a Dumb Surfer Dude 2: For the Love of Logan
Just a Dumb Surfer Dude 3: Summer Hearts
Gavin's Big Gay Checklist
A Surplus of Light
GINJUH
When Words Grow Fangs
Sending Love Letters to Animals and Other Totally Normal Human Behaviors

LGBTQ+ New Adult/Lit Fic/MM Romance

The Bees and Other Wild Things (sequel to *A Surplus of Light*)
A Tremendous Amount of Normal
The Gravity of Nothing
Between Enzo & the Universe
The Warmth of Our Closest Star
A Straight Line (w/ co-author J.D. Wade)

LGBTQ+ Magical Realism

Possibly Texas

A Point Worth LGBTQ Paranormal Romances

Jacob Michaels Is Tired (Book 1)
Jacob Michaels Is Not Crazy (Book 2)
Jacob Michaels Is Not Jacob Michaels (Book 3)
Jacob Michaels Is Not Here (Book 4)
Jacob Michaels Is Trouble (Book 5)
CARNAVAL (A Point Worth LGBTQ Paranormal Romance Story)
Jacob Michaels Is Dead (Book 6)
Jacob Michaels Is… The Omnibus Edition (all 6 JMI books and CARNAVAL)

Head Rock Harbor Mystery series

Head for Murder (Book 1)
Murder in the Rough (Book 2)

Erotica

Bully
Briefly Buddies
Jake (A Novella from Tricked: The Men of Briefly Buddies)
Tricked: The Men of Briefly Buddies eBook

Audiobooks

A Surplus of Light: A Gay Coming-of-Age Tale (narrated by Brian Lore Evans)
Between Enzo & the Universe (narrated by Brian Lore Evans; Tantor Media)

Translated

Between Enzo & the Universe – **Spanish**
A Surplus of Light – **Spanish**

Dedicated To:

Dr. R. and Officer J. as always
and
the readers who making writing even more magical.

Contents

Chapter One

Sawyer's boat was typical for a regular citizen of Head Rock Harbor, meaning it was a basic 18-foot Jon boat with a 60-horsepower outboard motor for open water and a 24v trolling motor for the shallows. Unlike other boats in town, Sawyer had taken the time to install a padded high-back folding boat seat for himself at the back and had added vinyl-covered padding to all of the other bench seats. My tailbone was thanking him as we sliced through and bobbed on the choppy waters of Old Man River. The fact that he kept his boat clean and in immaculate condition had the fussy side of me thanking him as well.

"*Whoooooooooooop!*" Sawyer hooted as the boat crested and flopped over a particularly impressive wave.

As the bow slammed back onto the Mississippi, ice-cold water sprayed over the bow and spritzed my face. I pulled my jacket more tightly around myself. Thinking about having a face full of Mississippi River water made my nose turn up. I shot a look over my shoulder at Sawyer and he laughed. It was late April, crawling towards May, but the water still felt like we'd just abandoned winter. The wind felt like pinpricks on my neck and face, especially when combined with the water spray from the river.

Fortunately, between the wind and the choppiness of the river, Sawyer finally realized that his joyful recklessness was leading to danger. He let up on the throttle and brought us down to a speed where we were slicing through the waves as opposed to hurdling them. My stomach grumbled as it settled back into its regular place in my gut.

"*Sorry!*" Sawyer shouted as the boat slowed, then reverted to a normal speaking voice once our speed evened out. "Just had to have a little fun."

"When you asked me to come with you, I thought it would be less stressful than avoiding Charlene," I said. "Now I see that I have chosen poorly."

Chuckling, Sawyer said, "Nah. It's fine. I was just excited to be back out on the river. I won't get you hurt. I swear."

"I'd appreciate it."

I reached up and ran my fingers through my brown curls—which were surely frizzing—wondering how much I resembled a drowned rat. For being a resident of Head Rock Harbor, I'm not keen on the cult of the river. As a concept, it's nice. Walking along the shores and taking in the views, sitting and staring out at the passing boats, and catching sights of wildlife—that interests me. The water may be brown, but it's still somehow beautiful. However, the boat culture of Head Rock Harbor wasn't ingrained in my DNA as it was with most of the population.

Though I had absolutely nothing against my fellow Head Rock Harbor citizens who practically worshipped the river during the warmer months, I was more of a passive river lover. Though I'd never refer to myself as "outdoorsy," I also wouldn't call myself a strictly indoors type of guy, either. I enjoyed the outdoors. However, I preferred activities that kept me out of the muck and away from danger. A nice hike in the woods? Wonderful. Hurtling over waves of muddy water in an aluminum boat at thirty miles per hour? Not my cup of tea.

Then again, risking life and limb in an open-air tin coffin was preferable to church. Which was how I'd found myself in Sawyer's boat out on the Mississippi looking for illegal trotlines to cut. Charlene had accosted me on Saturday afternoon in the shop, informing me that she was taking me to church the next day, and then out to lunch. Apparently, we had *a lot to discuss* about the Harbor Street Business Owners Association. Since I was not an avid member, nor had I expressed any interest in being involved in the HSBOA, I had no idea what we could possibly have to discuss.

So, when Sawyer had texted that evening and asked if I wanted to go out on his boat with him the next day, I'd practically leapt at the opportunity. Staying at home, in my pajamas, and watching something trashy on T.V. while curled up in bed with Rattlesnatches would have been best. Forced to choose between church and the river—I took the river. Rattlesnatches and T.V. would be waiting once Sawyer took me back home. Whenever that time came.

"City Council told everyone to have their lines pulled by the fifteenth," Sawyer announced as he let up on the motor, the deafening roar suddenly a murmur. "But Marv says that people have been spotting plenty over the last few days."

"Why didn't Marv send Jeremy or Ashley to come out here and yank 'em?" I asked, turning to straddle the bench to talk now that it was safe.

"Don't take away my side hustles, man," Sawyer chuckled. "The city's paying me to come out here and cut these lines."

I laughed with him.

"I guess if you're dying to do it, I have no objections," I said.

"I saved you from church." Sawyer reminded me. "Show a little gratitude."

Chuckling, I gazed at the trees lining the shore as we puttered along the river. Even though I'd joined Sawyer on his boat to avoid Charlene, I was still expected to help. Two pairs of eyes looking out for the tell-tale signs of heavy fishing line leading out of the water was better than one. Even though trotlines use heavier fishing line than what you'd find on a fishing pole, it's still nearly invisible against the movement of the water and the camouflage of the trees and their wind-rustled leaves. With both Sawyer's and my eyes watching, we had a better chance of catching all of the illegal lines.

"So," I asked, "what happens if we find any?"

"We yank 'em up, check the snoods, free any fish, and pull up the lines to toss when we get back to town," Sawyer explained.

"How do we know who put the line out?"

"We don't." Sawyer sounded deflated. "That's the worst part."

"So, we don't get to give Marv names of people to give tickets to?" I asked, smiling over at Sawyer. "This is boring."

Sawyer chuckled, but I could see in his face that he agreed. Finding illegal trotlines that were set to catch fish after the allowed dates and having no one to punish was annoying. When people break the law—especially when it involves protecting animals—some form of punishment is best. Knowing people would get off without so much as a ticket was irksome. Then again, a lot of people fished to feed their families, so I found myself with an ethical conundrum.

I decided to push my feelings away and focus on finding the lines to cut.

We puttered along the river, ten yards from the shore, for a while, our eyes focused on finding any lines. For a while, I figured we were simply wasting our time. When the City Council tells Marv to send someone out to cut illegal lines, word spreads quickly. It was possible that all of the people who had set lines had already harvested and cut the lines before we'd gotten on the river. However, the smallest flash of orange caught my eye suddenly.

"Got one!" I announced, pointing towards the shore.

Tied around the low-hanging branch of a cottonwood was the tiniest sliver of orange fabric. Next to it, a nearly invisible line ran down into the water. If it hadn't been for the person who set the line marking the spot to make it easier for them to find it, I wouldn't have known it was there. Fortunately, a fisherman making concessions for his poor memory landed me the first spotting of an illegal line.

"You lucked out," Sawyer said. "That one's tagged."

"Still in the lead," I replied. "'S'not my fault you missed it."

Grumbling playfully, Sawyer directed us toward the shallows. In the flat-bottomed Jon boat, it was easy for Sawyer to get us right up to the branch of the tree. He had to pull the motor up to keep from getting stuck in the viscous Mississippi mud. We'd probably have to use the oars to push back out into deeper water so we could put the motor back down. However, we didn't have to get out of the boat and get wet and muddy. That's all that mattered to me.

I watched as Sawyer grabbed the tree limb and used physical force to pull the boat into position next to the trotline. Working quickly, he used his pocketknife to snip the line, then deftly began pulling it into the boat. Every two to three feet, we'd find a snood—a smaller line hanging off the main line with a baited hook attached. Fortunately, even though the trotline was fairly long, none of the hooks had fish attached. Several had lost their bait—either to the water or clever fish—but none had caught anything.

"One down," Sawyer said.

He had curled the line up like a lasso by his feet and was readjusting himself in his seat.

"You want to pass me a beer?" he asked, pointing at the cooler next to my bench seat.

"Sure," I said.

I opened the Igloo Playmate cooler—an honest-to-goodness red and white Igloo Playmate cooler—and fetched a can of Pabst Blue Ribbon for Sawyer. Smiling, he caught the beer that I tossed him, and opened it immediately, ignoring the spritz of foam. Laughing at him, I pulled a soda out of the cooler and popped the tab.

"You're up," Sawyer said, nodding at the oars.

Groaning, I put my soda can between my knees, holding it tightly, and grabbed an oar. Leaning over a bit, I pushed the oar into the water next to us until I felt resistance, and pushed away from the mushy floor of the river. I held onto the oar handle like a vice since the mud did its best to suck it out of my grip. The boat drifted away from shore and I yanked the oar out of the mud. I gave it a twirl in the water to rinse off, then pulled it back into the boat to lay alongside the hull once more.

Sawyer gave me an approving nod, then dropped the trolling motor once we had drifted out far enough. He started the motor up and we were puttering away again, sipping our drinks as we watched the trees on the shore like hawks.

Over the next hour, Sawyer found two more lines and I found one, keeping us tied in score and making us both search harder for trotlines. There was no prize for finding the most lines, but the competitive nature of us both kept the game exciting. By the time we were tied two to two, we were not speaking to each other, focusing solely on spotting lines. The game was afoot and we were playing as though our lives depended upon it.

Sawyer was on his third beer—*I had no intention of tattling to Marv*—and I was on my second soda when Sawyer spotted the fifth illegal trotline.

"*Whoooooooop!*" Sawyer hollered again.

Pumping a fist in the air, he finally pointed to the line that he spotted tied to a stake on the shore. We had been rounding a bend, an anabranch in the river, when he'd spotted the line.

"That's not fair," I demanded playfully. "We were coming around the bend."

"You're at the front of the boat, man!" Sawyer laughed, pointing out my advantage.

I merely shot him a smile over my shoulder, letting him know there were no hard feelings, and the trolling motor sputtered, easing us toward the shore. Sawyer was still chuckling, proud of his keen eyesight as he aimed us towards the shore. Seeing his chest puffed out so proudly made me want to grab a handful of ice from the cooler to chuck at him—*in a playful way, of course*—but I somehow managed to ignore the intrusive thought.

We were barely ten feet from the shore when the trolling motor sputtered and kicked, lifting out of the water. With an incredibly Midwestern "ope," Sawyer caught it, switching it off as he simultaneously nestled it in the upright position out of the water. A second later, the bow of the boat bumped into the muddy bottom of the river and the boat shuddered.

"I'm not getting in the mud," I said immediately.

Sawyer laughed.

"Seriously," I said. "You're getting paid for this. Not me."

I joined him in laughing.

"Well," Sawyer said, reaching up to rub his chin, "we're not that far out. And the riverbed is mush right up to the shore right now. The water's probably just high enough. We can probably use the oars to push up to the shore and hop out onto dry land. Then we can push away with the oars after we get the line pulled up."

"Sounds reasonable," I said, reaching for an oar. "I need to answer Mother Nature's call anyway."

"Agreed," Sawyer burped. "The PBRs are doing their job."

"Classy," I quipped.

Laughing, Sawyer grabbed the other oar. In unison, me on the right and him on the left, we pushed the oars through the shallow water, down into the riverbed, and pushed towards shore. When the bow of the Jon boat bumped the shore, it got lodged into the mud enough to keep us from floating away. Sawyer and I pulled the oars back into the boat and scrambled carefully out of the boat onto shore.

Before addressing the trotline or the call of nature, Sawyer tied the boat off on a nearby tree limb. You could never be too careful. With the boat in the shallows and the mud cradling its bottom, it was unlikely to drift away. However, the possibility was undesirable enough that precautions had to be taken. I waited patiently for Sawyer to secure the boat, stretching my arms and legs at his side.

"That should do it," he said. "If you want to go take care of business, I'll take care of the trotline first."

"Sounds good." I agreed.

Turning to walk away from Sawyer, I got a sudden flash of an idea of where we were on the river.

"Hey," I turned back to Sawyer, "is that the Wilford Woods?"

Jabbing a thumb over my shoulder towards the woods off from the shore, Sawyer turned to look where I was pointing. He squinted his eyes and considered my question for a moment, then nodded.

"You're right," Sawyer said.

"Jeremy and I used to hike the trail through there all the time back in high school," I said. "Opens out right behind the trailer park."

"Well," Sawyer laughed, "I'd rather use the boat. That's a good two miles from here and I don't think I have the hike in me after three beers."

I agreed with a chuckle. Silently, I stepped away and left Sawyer to deal with the trotline. I didn't have to go far to find a large tree for privacy. The woods were a mere ten yards away from the shore. Quickly, I set about doing my business. Once done and decent again, I moved away from the tree and turned to head back to meet Sawyer at the shore.

As I was turning, a flash of orange caught my eye, and I stopped to stare into the woods. How I'd missed it walking over to the tree, I couldn't figure, but the bright orange fabric deeper in the woods was obviously a tent. Frowning, I stared into the woods at the tent out in the middle of nowhere.

It wasn't uncommon for people to camp out in Wilford Woods, a secluded area at the south end of town. Jeremy and I had camped a few times back in our school days. It was close enough to town that if we had an emergency, one of us could run for help quickly, but it was far enough away that it felt like we were kind of roughing it. However, since there was a trotline staked to the shore, I had to wonder if the person camping twenty yards away was the owner.

"Got the line pulled up." Sawyer's voice a few feet behind me made me jump. "Two fish. Got 'em thrown back."

Spinning to find Sawyer grinning at my jumpy reaction, I jabbed a thumb over my shoulder.

"Someone's camping out here," I said.

Squinting, Sawyer leaned to look over my shoulder.

"Looks like it," he said with a nod. "Probably the jackwagon that put the trotline out."

I nodded. "That's what I'm thinking."

Shaking his head, Sawyer moved to put his back to me and sidled up to the tree.

"Let me answer this call and we'll go check it out," he said.

"All right."

I turned my back to give Sawyer privacy and stared out into the woods at the neon orange tent peeking out between the trees. No smoke was rising from the area of the campsite and I didn't hear any voices drifting through the woods. Of course, the woods were dense so it was possible that if the campers were being quiet, we wouldn't hear them out by the shore. Other than the tent I couldn't see any signs of life, though.

Typically, you'd see people moving around a campsite, smoke rising from a fire, voices of people talking and having a good time, and maybe some music if the campers were fancy. However, the woods were quiet. All I could hear was the sound of Sawyer answering Mother Nature's call behind me. When I heard the tell-tale zipping sound, signaling that he was done, I turned back to face him.

"Well," he said, pulling his shirt down over the front of his jeans, "should we go check it out?"

I shrugged.

"I don't know," I said. "I don't see anyone out there. And if they don't care about fishing laws, they're probably not going to be super happy if we show up to chew them out about it."

Sawyer thought about that for a moment.

"We don't know how many people might be out here." He agreed.

"Right."

"It's probably local kids," he said with finality, then pushed away from the tree. "Let's go give them a scare. Make 'em think they're getting in big trouble."

Sawyer's devilish grin made me chuckle and I fell into step beside him warily.

"But if it's not," I began, hustling alongside him, "and it's some guy out here with a bunch of guns, I'm going to be really mad at you if we get shot."

Sawyer laughed as we began to walk through the woods. After a few yards through the growth, Sawyer leaned his head back and hollered.

"*Anyone out here?*" he bellowed.

We continued to stomp through the brush, dodging tree limbs as we made our way closer to the orange tent and the campsite. I had expected to hear a voice holler back at us, or at least see a head poke up through the trees, searching for the source of Sawyer's voice. However, the campsite remained still and quiet as a churchyard as we approached. Sawyer shot me a glance and a shrug, which I returned.

Moments later, we were pushing through the last bit of brush and stepping into the small clearing in the woods where the unknown campers had set up. Though obviously having been in use, the campsite was presently unoccupied. The flaps at the opening were tied back and a quick glance inside the tent showed it to be empty.

Though I didn't want to disrupt other people's belongings, I pushed back the flap of the tent to get a better look into the tent. Everything seemed in place for a campsite. Two sleeping bags set up that could accommodate one person apiece, a little table with a battery-operated lantern, a bag that probably contained fresh clothes and toiletries—the usual camping accouterments. Nothing out of the usual, but nobody was inside of the tent.

Around the campsite, it looked as though a fresh fire hadn't been lit recently. The firepit was full of ashes and when I knelt to put my hand near the center, no warmth radiated from it. No lingering smoldering embers flickered. Two camp chairs were set near the firepit, facing it, and a large chest cooler was between the chairs. It was either for easy access to drinks or for the dual function of also providing additional seating. That made it impossible to tell how many people had been, or were, using the campsite.

"No one here," Sawyer said.

I made a non-committal sound with my throat. The two of us looked around the clearing, but it was futile.

"They probably went for a hike. Or maybe they are out on their boat?" Sawyer suggested.

Nodding along, it was possible the camper—or campers—had gone for a hike through the woods. It was also possible they had come to the campsite by boat and were currently out enjoying the river. Whatever the case, there was no one to ask about the illegal trotline at the moment. However, if they had come to the campsite by boat, it made it more likely that they had set the trotline.

"I think that—"

Before I could finish my thought, my wandering eyes fell on a pair of boots sticking out from behind a tree at the edge of the campsite. Frowning, I wondered why anyone would set their boots so far away from the tent.

"What?" Sawyer asked.

Not responding verbally, I gestured for him to follow me. Sawyer fell in step behind me as I crossed the campsite, walking the few yards between the tent and the tree.

"What are those doing there?" Sawyer asked as we approached the tree. "That's a weird spot to put boots."

When we rounded the tree, there was no need to give my take on the strange spot where the boots had been left.

Because there was a pair of legs coming out of the boots. Most importantly, there was a whole body attached to those legs. And that body was staring up at the trees above, lifeless and unseeing. The obvious shotgun blast chest wound and blood-stained shirt of the man told us all we needed to know. A shotgun lay two yards away, partially covered by leaves.

Wind whistled through the campsite as Sawyer and I stared down at the dead body.

"You can have the credit for finding this trotline," Sawyer said quietly.

Chapter Two

Sitting in the dead man's camping chairs felt disrespectful, but Sawyer and I did as instructed by Marv. Chief Marvin "Marv" Bucksworth had immediately gone about securing the scene and taking charge upon his arrival. Being a mere few minutes' walking distance into the woods outside of town, it didn't take long for the police to arrive. Sawyer had immediately called 911 after we found the man's body. He spoke with the dispatcher, Gloria, for a few moments, then dropped our GPS coordinates to the police department via his phone.

Jeremy was the first to show up. Finding Sawyer and I standing over a dead body gave my best friend—and Head Rock Harbor detective—pause. Fortunately, Officer Ashley Riley and Marv were less than two minutes behind him. Trying to explain ourselves multiple times to different people would have been annoying at best and ineffective at worst. Having to explain to Jeremy why Sawyer and I were out on the river together would have been uncomfortable as well. I wasn't sure why, though.

So, Marv instructed Sawyer and I to "take a load off" in the two canvas and aluminum camping chairs set up by the fire pit. With Officer Riley's and Jeremy's assistance, he examined the body of the man behind the tree. Though we knew better than to talk too much, Sawyer and I exchanged furtive glances and shrugs. Neither of us knew what had happened to the man, but we knew that he was incredibly dead. Furthermore, both of us were smart enough to figure out the cause of death since the shotgun blast wound, and the shotgun itself, were present.

"*Suicide?*" Sawyer whispered out of the corner of his mouth.

"*Maybe?*" I whispered back.

Other than that quick exchange, we said nothing more. Instead, the two of us listened carefully as Marv, Jeremy, and Ashley spoke over the body with hushed tones. All three crouched around the body and pointed out things they noticed about the body to each other. With the wind whistling through the trees and the sound of the river, it was nearly impossible to catch more than every tenth word or so. Finally, I gave up and relaxed in my chair, staring out into the woods blankly.

For obvious reasons, it crossed my mind that this was the second dead body I'd discovered in so many months. Obviously, I took comfort in the fact that I was not alone for my second dead body. Without Sawyer, Marv and his guys probably would have been looking at me sideways. Sawyer's presence meant the three of them focused on investigating the scene instead. Of course, Jeremy might have given me the benefit of the doubt. Best friends do that.

Officer Riley and Marv might not have been so kind, though. Any cop worth his salt would find it odd that a person found two dead bodies in two months. At the very least, they'd ask a few more questions than they would of a typical witness. A month earlier, I'd been the person to find Marshelle Martin's car and her dead body out by The Bluff. I didn't need to make this a habit.

Absently, I reached over and lifted the lid of the cooler between mine and Sawyer's chairs. Bottles of water, cans of soda, some lunch meat, and a Styrofoam container with an opaque lid that looked like it came from a bait shop lay amongst mostly melted ice. "Nelson" was written in big, bold letters in permanent marker on the underside of the lid. I stared down at the contents for a few moments before lowering the lid silently. I gave it a solid press to make sure that it was sealed well.

"I guess it's obvious," Marv said, waking me from my daydream as he walked over, crunching twigs and leaves, "that the man's been shot."

Sawyer and I both looked up simultaneously, though neither of us replied to the chief.

"Pretty close range I'd say, too," Marv added. "Bit of blood on the barrel of the shotgun. Pretty decent entry wound…well, gruesome to say the least. You boys all right?"

Sawyer and I glanced at each other.

Nodding, I said, "A little shaken, but okay, I guess."

Sawyer nodded along.

Marv's mouth tightened sympathetically as he looked down at us, then he glanced over his shoulder before giving us a serious look.

"Y'all didn't see or hear nothing?" he asked.

"Nothing," Sawyer said.

"We stopped to cut a trotline—like we were supposed to be doing—took a second to, uh, use the bathroom, and we saw the campsite here," I explained. "We came to check it out and…found him."

Marv squinted at me. "What made you feel you needed to come check it out?"

"We thought the owner of the tent might also be the owner of the trot line," I said, which turned Marv's squint into a grin. "We were going to find out who it was so we could give a name to you so you could ticket them."

"Spook 'em at least," Sawyer added. "So they didn't fish illegally again. Or think twice before doing it again."

Marv chuckled. "Makes sense. I know you boys are clear. Don't need the forensics team to tell me that. This fella's been dead since last night. Don't need forensics for that, either. Seeing that I saw you both having breakfast at Munchie's this morning, I think you're clear."

"We could have killed him last night. You didn't see us then," I said.

"Do you want to be a murder suspect?" Marv frowned at me.

"No," I said. "Just making a point."

"Stop making points," Sawyer punched me lightly in the knee.

The three of us laughed, though it was restrained. There was a dead guy a few yards away, after all. Marv cleared his throat and heaved a sigh before shaking his head ruefully.

"Well," he said, "you boys can take off. I know where I can find both of you if I have more questions. Do the right thing and keep this to yourselves, all right?"

He pointed a stern finger at us.

"Sure thing," Sawyer said, rising from his chair. "You think it's suicide? He was out here all alone, right? Close range shot? Maybe he came out here to end it all, Marv."

Marv shrugged. "As good a theory as any at the moment. But we won't jump to any conclusions until the science nerds get out here and collect evidence."

Rising from my chair, a frown plastered itself to my face. Sawyer shrugged and headed off towards the river. Marv saw the look on my face and turned to face me, crossing his arms over his chest. Confused, I looked around the campsite.

"You're thinking," Marv snorted.

I didn't respond.

"Let's hear it, Jackson," he said with a chuckle. "May as well get your thoughts out now so you won't feel the need to keep thinking about it. What's got your dander up?"

"Out here alone?" I questioned. "Why are there two camp chairs?"

Marv looked down at the chairs as though he'd never seen them before.

"Was he planning to entertain or something?" I asked.

With a chuckle, Marv met my eyes again.

"Who's to say?" he responded.

"Fair enough," I said.

Marv wasn't being dismissive, nor was he not following my thought process. He simply wasn't going to share his thoughts with me. I couldn't blame the guy. Certainly, the chief of police would have to be a fool to give any information—including his investigative process—to a civilian. Because I noticed something he had not didn't mean he had to share anything about the scene or the crime with me. I wasn't employed by the police department.

"Just seems odd," I added.

Marv nodded. "You go on with Sawyer. We've got it from here."

"Got it."

I started to walk away, had another thought invade my mind, and turned back to Marv after a few steps. Marv dropped his arms to his sides and squinted at me.

"I know, I know." I held my hands up defensively. "I didn't recognize him. Did you?"

Marv shook his head after a moment of considering his options.

"He might be related to the Nelsons. You know—Mason, Hunter, Kenny, and Myrna?" I said before gesturing at the cooler. "The name 'Nelson' is written inside the lid."

Marv glowered at me.

"Okay," I said, backing away, my hands held out again.

"You touch anything else?" he grumbled.

"No," I said. "I don't think so. Well, the tent flap when we looked inside before we found him."

Marv was shaking his head and then began waving me away with annoyance.

"Go."

The one word was enough for me. Marv's tone told me all I needed to hear. I turned and began to briskly walk towards the river to join Sawyer at his boat. Only once did I glance over my shoulder, but Marv had turned around and walked back to the body. Jeremy was looking after me, his brow furrowed and his eyes dark. I turned my head back around and dashed through the woods and back out to the river.

Sawyer had already thrown the rolled-up trotline in his boat and was climbing in when I approached him on the shore of the river. Something in my gut was bothering me. An idea I couldn't quite stop from swirling around in my brain long enough to examine. Of course, when you stumble across a dead body—especially one so gruesome—it does strange things to the brain. Everything back at the campsite could have been perfectly normal. As normal as any death site could be, anyway. It was possible my brain was simply jarred by the discovery of the body with a giant wound in its chest.

"You getting in?" Sawyer asked.

"Yeah," I said, shaking my head. "Sorry."

Climbing carefully from the shore into the boat, I took up my position on the bench seat in the middle of the boat and grabbed an oar. Sawyer grabbed the other oar and we worked together to push ourselves far enough away from the bank of the river so that he could drop the motor. Once we'd pushed out to a safe distance, the two of us rinsed the mud off our oars and laid them along the side of the boat. Sawyer lowered the motor with a sigh.

"That's not how I expected my morning to go," he said.

"Yeah." I agreed. "I'm tired of finding dead bodies. And that's only the second one I've personally found."

Sawyer didn't say anything for a moment, nor did he start the motor. I glanced over my shoulder. He was staring at me.

"What?" I chuckled nervously. "I didn't do it."

"I know. It's just…that was weird, right?"

"The body? Yeah."

"No," he said. "Germ, man. He was a little frosty, right?"

My gut gave me another signal that was easier to interpret than the one in my brain.

"I mean," I answered slowly, "he's dealing with a potential crime scene. He's not going to be all rainbows and sunshine, right?"

Sawyer nodded slowly and glanced towards the woods again.

"I guess so," he said. "He sure didn't like finding us out here together."

Frowning, I said, "What's that supposed to mean?"

Before I could say anything else, Sawyer grinned devilishly.

"Nothing," he said. "Germ can just be a weird guy, I guess."

Nodding slowly, I finally answered, "Yeah. Sometimes."

Sawyer suddenly started up the engine, making me jump. Laughing loudly at my reaction, he grabbed the tiller handle and aimed us towards open water. He gave the throttle a twist and we sped out into the river. Turning to sit properly on the bench, I faced the bow of the boat and stared out at the water as the boat sliced through it.

The spray of the cold river water wasn't nearly as startling as it had been at the start of the morning. I didn't know if that meant I was running on adrenaline, in shock, or confused by what Sawyer had said. Regardless of the reason, I was ready to be out of the boat, off of the river, and back on dry land once more.

I wanted to go home and shower.

Twice.

Chapter Three

Head Rock Harbor Books makes me think of a library more than it does a bookstore. Not because I have rules about "inside voices" and late fees posted at the door. It's because the check-out counter, the stairs leading up to my apartment, the balcony, the bookshelves, and the floors are all original, solid wood. Beautifully finished dark wood that would look more at home in a university library than it would a bookstore, it's a gorgeous space.

Though the main store space isn't exceptionally large for a bookstore, it still feels cavernous. Due to the two-story ceiling over half of the store and the depth of the building, it almost feels as though you could get lost looking for a book. It's a ridiculous thought; how could anyone get physically lost in a bookstore? However, with the tall shelves that barely allow their tops to be cleaned with a feather duster when I'm standing on tiptoes, it's easy to believe it's possible.

If you're searching the science fiction shelf, for example, you can look to one end and see the check-out counter. At the other end, you can see the opposite wall of the store, lined with manga, comic books, and magazines. However, unless there is someone else in the aisle with you, you will feel entirely alone in the store. The tall, full shelves create a cocoon of silence that feels as though you're wearing earmuffs. All other noise in the store feels like it's being relayed through water.

When I first took over the store and was getting it ready for reopening, I found runner carpets in warm greens, oranges, maroons, and browns to line the aisles between shelves. More ran from the front door to the check-out counter, and from the check-out counter to the stairs. Of course, the carpet was not to invite people to venture upstairs. That's where my private residence was, after all. However, the space felt bare without that extra rug. Protecting the hardwood floors was a bonus. In East Central Iowa, Head Rock Harbor Books hosts many customers with outdoor wear that is harmful to finished wood.

I didn't bother to turn on the store lights when I got home. Sawyer dropped me off in front of the store when we got back from the river. We hadn't bothered to look for any more trotlines after finding the body in the woods. Instead, Sawyer had taken us right back to the boat ramp, loaded his boat up onto his trailer, and took me home. He could tell from the look on my face that our game of "spot the illegal trotlines" had gotten old.

Once he was certain I'd gotten the front door of the shop unlocked, he gave me a wave from the cab of his truck and drove off. The boat on his trailer bounced behind him as he headed out. I locked the front door behind me and leaned back against the front door, making sure the frame took my weight as to protect the glass panes.

"*Mew.*"

The mewling drew my attention to the interior balcony outside of my small second-floor apartment. His angular head stuck between the balusters of the balcony, two triangle ears perked up, Rattlesnatches was staring inquisitively down at me. With his head cocked to the side and his eyes twinkling in the darkness of the shop, I felt home sloughing away the tension of the morning.

"Another dead body," I said to my cat. "Out in Wilford Woods."

"*Mew.*"

"That's what I was thinking."

When I pushed away from the door and headed to the stairs, Rattlesnatches' head disappeared from between the balusters. We met again when I ascended the stairs and headed across the length of the balcony to my apartment door. I'd left it open so that Rattlesnatches had access to all areas of the store while I was out on the river. Being locked up was a surefire way to put him in a bad mood, and that's always best avoided whenever possible.

My presence upstairs put Rattlesnatches at ease and he dashed into my apartment, obviously ready for snuggle time. I'd barely begun to kick my shoes off next to the easy chair placed outside my apartment door when my cellphone rang in my pocket. Holding onto the chair back for support as I kicked off my shoes, I pulled my phone out of my pocket. Jeremy's name and picture were plastered on the screen, so I immediately swiped to answer.

"What's up, Germ?" I asked, keeping my tone casual.

"Have you washed your hands or taken a shower yet?" he asked.

His tone was not as casual.

"Not yet," I said. "Just got home."

"Sawyer drop you off?"

"Well…yeah?"

Silence pervaded for a moment, then Jeremy finally began to speak again.

"We're sending a forensic tech by to do a GSR test on your hands," he explained. *"Don't wash up until he gets there."*

I assumed he meant Deacon, the newest—and first—forensic tech to work for Head Rock Harbor Police Department. He was a cousin of a cousin of our illustrious mayor, Linda Wagner. When Deacon graduated and became certified, there was suddenly a vote to add a budget for a forensics tech to the department. Of course, it caused grumblings in the community for a few months, but since everyone actually liked Deacon, the hubbub died off quickly enough.

"Okay," I said, shrugging to myself. It only made sense that Marv and the boys would cover all their bases. Though, it would have made more sense to have us wait at the scene instead of letting us leave. "Do you need me to—"

"I gotta go," Jeremy said abruptly. *"I hope I can get ahold of Sawyer before he washes up from your morning activities."*

When the line went dead suddenly, I pulled my phone away from my ear and my brow furrowed as I stared down at the icons on the screen. Jeremy had pulled the most popular movie and television blunder. He hadn't even said "goodbye."

With a sigh, I locked my phone and slid it back into my pocket. Since a shower and a nap was out of the question for the time being, I headed back downstairs, unlocked the front door, and flipped on the store lights. I took up a position on the stool behind the check-out counter and jiggled the mouse to wake up the computer.

Though I try to not make it a habit to use the bookstore computer to do business that isn't, well, business, I didn't want to walk upstairs and get my laptop. After a harrowing and gut-churning image search, I decided that what the internet had on display as a typical close-range gunshot wound was similar to what we'd seen earlier in the day.

Fingers hovering over the keys and staring off into space, I tried to make the thoughts swirling through my head slow down. Whatever was tickling my gray matter was impossible to pluck from the vortex in my brain. All I could picture was the gunshot hole in the man's chest, his bruise-colored face, and his mouth twisted open in horror.

The sorrow and pain a person had to feel in the moments before they took their life had to be harrowing. I shuddered at the thought of a poor soul out in the woods, alone, trying to position a gun perfectly against their chest to end their life. How deeply desperate a person had to feel to decide that there was only one solution to whatever problems they were facing in life. It didn't feel good to know that someone had died alone and so horrifically.

"*Ugh.*" The word came out with a great gust of breath.

I put the computer back to sleep and shook my head in an attempt to clear it of thoughts. The dead body in the woods was a problem for the Head Rock Harbor Police Department. Not the owner of Head Rock Harbor Books.

It crossed my mind to check the shelves and organize books that might need it, but I didn't know if that would affect the GSR test. Gun shot residue tests, though not completely foreign to me, were still not within my expertise. Though no one besides my agent and publisher knew it, I was the author of the bestselling *Detective Randy Melton Mystery series*.

Research and reading over the years for the series made me functionally familiar with gunshot residue tests. I knew to expect the forensic tech to show up, swab my hands, put the swabs in a sterile baggie, and then take them back to the lab for a bath in a nitric acid solution. This helped separate all of the elements the swabs picked up on my hands. Microscopes or other tools would then be utilized for analysis. Thus, it could be determined if I had recently shot a gun, handled explosives—or any of the organic or inorganic matter that was found in either.

Thankfully, I knew my test would come back negative. Unless they started to look for traces of Mississippi River water or fish guts.

However, my nerves were still raw. Waiting for a tech to come perform a GSR test was like going to a laboratory to give a urine sample for an employer's drug test. Even if you know you're innocent, maybe you somehow accidentally fired a gun. Or shot a syringe full of heroin between your toes.

The perpetually innocent and pathologically boring person often worries about their mentally fabricated guilt.

When the bell over the front door clanged, I nearly fell off of my stool.

Deacon Davis was stepping through the front door of Head Rock Harbor Books, grinning devilishly at me.

"Did I spook you?" he asked.

"Sorry," I said. "I was just lost in thought. I didn't see you walk up."

He waved me off. "I was going to knock, but I figured that was a strange thing to do at a bookstore, right?"

I chuckled. "Of course."

Deacon Davis, barely old enough to have gotten a college degree, certification, and training, was the youngest employee of Head Rock Harbor Police Department. His white-blond hair, rail-thin build, slight stature, and youthful, hairless face did nothing to help the matter. Both angular and soft at the same time, his face caused everyone to question his abilities whenever he reported to work. He had the softness of youth combined with the angles of a guy who recently lost his baby fat. The fact that I, along with many other men in town, stood a head taller than him completely finished him off.

"Jeremy said he called?" Deacon asked, swinging a pack off of his shoulder and laying it gently on the check-out counter.

"Yeah," I said. "I haven't washed my hands or showered yet."

"Then we're granola."

"I'm sorry?" I cocked my head to the side. "What?"

"*Ready to go.*" Deacon looked up at me and winked as he dug through his bag. "We can hit the trail. Get to the hike. Get moving. Start—"

"Got it," I said with a chuckle.

"Just swinging some new slang."

"The best slang doesn't require an explanation."

"Tell me the last time you heard the teens talk and didn't need a dictionary," he said, his eyes twinkling as he pulled a small box from his pack.

I shrugged.

"Like I said, slang that needs an explanation is bad," I explained. "The slang nowadays sucks."

Deacon laughed heartily, but the sound coming out of his delicate mouth didn't sound right. It was infectious, either way. Ignoring the box momentarily, he dug in his pack and pulled out a plastic hazardous materials baggie. My gut churned.

When was the last time I handled a gun?

"Have you been hunting or anything recently?" Deacon asked as he flipped open a small notepad and extracted a pen from his pack.

"I don't remember the last time I held a gun," I said. "I don't hunt."

He nodded as if listening to a song only he could hear and jotted down a note.

"Handle any explosives?"

I laughed.

"No?" He didn't look up from his notepad, but he grinned.

"Big no."

"Fireworks?"

"No. Not since New Year's. And won't again until the Fourth of July."

More musical nodding.

"Change any brake pads?"

"Uh…no," I said. "I barely own a car."

It was true. My 1992 fire engine red Volkswagen Beetle was in decent enough shape. I made sure of that since I never skimped on maintenance. However, the fact that it was barely driven once a week made it less functional and more back-alley décor behind the shop.

"Allergic to latex?"

"Nope."

"We're not just granola, we're straight up trail mix," Deacon said as he looked up and grinned at me.

"Work on your material," I said.

Laughing, he stowed his notepad and pen in his pack, snapped on a pair of latex gloves, opened the little box and extracted two swabs. Holding one up in each hand, he grinned at me.

"You a righty or lefty?" he asked.

"Uh, lefty." I held my left hand up.

"I'm going to swab both, but it's best to know your dominant hand because—"

"That's the one I most likely used if I was shooting someone."

"Exactly."

"Doesn't a shotgun require *both* hands?" I asked.

"You sure know an awful lot about what's going on here," Deacon said, though I knew he was only teasing. "Do I need to take more notes?"

I rolled my eyes and laid both hands on the counter, palms up. Sensing my unease, Deacon reserved any further jokes and set to work swabbing both of my hands thoroughly. After swabbing my left hand, he meticulously dropped it in a baggie and sealed it shut. Then he moved on to my right hand. Within a matter of a minute, he had completed the task that Jeremy had sent him to do.

"All done with the swabs," Deacon said as he slipped the baggies into his pack.

He yanked his gloves off and held them out to me.

"Can you chuck these in your trash?"

I took the wadded-up gloves and tossed them in the trash under the check-out counter.

"That was as easy as I expected," I said, though my stomach was still in knots.

I expected it would stay knotted up until someone called to tell me that I was cleared of suspicion of murder.

"Quick and efficient," Deacon said. "That's me. Now I just need to bag up your clothes."

"Pardon?" I pulled back.

"Your clothes," Deacon said, gesturing vaguely at me. "I need to put them in a—"

He reached into his pack and extracted a piece of red plastic.

"—materials bag for testing later."

With a few flicks of his wrist, the piece of red plastic unfurled like a garbage bag.

"My...*clothes?*" I frowned.

He shrugged. "Could have gun powder on them. You might have lied and washed your hands and showered. You wouldn't have had time to wash your clothes yet, though."

My stomach knots twisted.

"I'll take them in, show them to Marv, he can confirm that's what you were wearing," Deacon explained, "then we'll test them. No worries. It's as simple as testing your hand swabs. Of course, you won't get the clothes back. But you wouldn't want them back."

"Uh, yeah, okay, I guess," I said. "I mean, I love this sweater—"

"Sorry," Deacon said.

"Let me just run upstairs and—"

"I have to observe," Deacon stopped me. "I can go up there with you if you don't want to strip down in the middle of the store."

If my stomach had been in knots before, it was absolutely tangled with this new discovery. I was going to have to strip down in front of Deacon Davis like a criminal. Was I going to be asked to do the ole *squat and cough* before it was all said and done? Shampoo my head and entire body with lice soap? Given an orange jumpsuit and flip flops? Handed a pile of linens?

"You get to keep your underwear," Deacon said, laughing at the obvious look of horror on my face. "Just the outer layers."

"Somehow that's better but not," I mumbled.

"Upstairs or here," Deacon said again. "But I can't let you go alone. Your choice, my friend. But Sawyer's waiting his turn, so don't dally."

I grumbled to myself and walked around the counter. Having Deacon up in my apartment felt too personal. It was bad enough he was going to see me out of clothes—I didn't want to make it any more intimate than necessary. Though it did cross my mind to tell Deacon to have Marv come back with a warrant. *Take my clothes? Come get 'em, you turd.*

"Just for the record, I don't have duplicates of all of my clothes," I said. "So, I couldn't pull a switcheroo on you."

Deacon laughed as I stepped into the aisle between the science fiction and horror shelves to put a barrier between me and the front windows of the shop. So that I didn't have time to think about it too much, I yanked off my sweater and the long-sleeve shirt underneath. Deacon was waiting when I tossed the ball of material to him, and he quickly deposited them in the red bag. I pulled my cellphone, keys, and wallet out of my jeans pockets and placed them on the shelf next to me. Taking a deep breath, I yanked off my jeans, stepped out of them, and tossed them to Deacon.

Professional and kind, Deacon kept his eyes down as he bagged up my pants and sealed the bag with a tie. Quickly, he slung the red bag over one shoulder and his pack of supplies over the other. Standing there in my boxer briefs, I knew there was nothing to say that would make the situation any less awkward. There was no obvious thing to say to Forensics Santa. But there was something I had to say.

"Twist the lock on the knob on your way out and get the lights, would you?" I asked. "I'm going to make a mad dash for the stairs once you're gone."

Deacon chuckled. "Sure thing."

He gave me a goodbye nod without looking up, then seconds later he disappeared from view. The lights went out a moment later, the door opened, the overhead bell clanged, and then the door shut. Tentatively, I glanced around the shelf to make sure that I was alone and no one was walking by outside.

Before I had a chance to dash for the stairs, a thought popped into my head. I snatched my phone off of the shelf and unlocked it.

Deacon will need your clothes. I shot off a quick text to Sawyer. *You might want to change before he gets there and have your clothes waiting to be collected.*

Almost immediately, I got a response.

Thanks for the heads up.

The wide-eyed emoji that accompanied the text made me chuckle.

After I locked my phone again, I glanced to the front of the store again. The coast was clear. I grabbed my belongings off the shelf and dashed across the store, up the stairs, across the balcony, and into my apartment.

Rattlesnatches was sitting on my bed, his eyes half shut with sleepiness. When he saw me, his eyes opened wide.

What exactly have you been up to? he seemed to say.

"Don't ask," I grumbled.

It was time for the two consecutive showers I'd had in mind when I got home.

Chapter Four

Fittingly, Head Rock Harbor is laid out similar to the letter H. Two perpendicular long roads running north to south from the bluff down to the where the river curves. However, instead of one line running through the center of the H, there are three. They run west to east. The northernmost, being Harbor Street, stops at the part of the river that runs on the east side of town. At the end of Harbor Street, you'll find the harbor and the main boat ramp in town. Which is also where Prescott Pemberton's naked body was found in early Spring. The middle street cuts through the center of downtown and stops at the river. The southernmost road cuts similarly through town, stopping at the river as well.

At the top of the H, you'll find the bluff, where all of the most affluent citizens of town have houses glaring down at the normies. At the southern legs of the H, you'll find the lower-class citizens of Head Rock Harbor. The Harper's Trailer Park, Harper's Bar, Grill, Bait & Tackle is there. As is Bernie's Tavern. Those kinds of places. However, the upscale restaurant, The Dock, is on the southern part of town. There's no real shady part of Head Rock Harbor since we're a small town with a population that has never gone over five thousand. However, there is a clear separation of upper- and lower-class citizens.

In the middle of the bottom two roads that cut west to east through town, you'll find the old town square. It's where all of the major town events occur, like the annual Halloween, Thanksgiving, and Christmas events. Special weekend events to attract tourists from the bigger cities will usually be found going on there, like the Fall Arts Festival.

So, maybe Head Rock Harbor is more like a section of a railroad track. An incredibly small section of railroad track. If you're swift footed, like me or any respectable gay man, you can walk from The Bluff down to Harper's Bar & Grill in five minutes flat. Head Rock Harbor Books is on the north side of the street, smack dab in the middle of Harbor Street. So, I can make it to Harper's on foot quickly.

Though I'd been reasonable and eaten leftovers for lunch after a thirty-minute scalding hot shower, for dinner I found myself at Harper's Bar, Grill, Bait & Tackle. The walk from the bookstore to the restaurant was chilly, yet uneventful. Fortunately, for a lazy, chilly Sunday, most of Head Rock Harbor's citizens had elected to stay indoors for the evening. That spared me small talk and questions.

The last time we'd had a dead body found—Prescott Pemberton, in the harbor, with the head wound—the town was abuzz with gossip within minutes. Less than a few days later, I'd been snagged to help deal with the dead man's property, and ultimately, nearly got stabbed to death— twice—in the process of solving his murder. With the new dead body, I was hoping to avoid all of the pomp and circumstance—and harrowing danger—and pretend it never happened.

Once I'd been cleared of suspicion by the GSR test, I was going to keep my head down. Even if everyone found out—*and they would*—that I was one of the two people who found the body, I'd refuse to answer questions. A simple shrug of the shoulders and a vacant tilt of my head would be my response. I was not in the business of murder. Neither committing nor solving.

The only murder and mystery I wanted to deal with were those my keys tapped out on my laptop.

Mental note to self, I thought to myself as I entered Harper's, *write a few pages tonight*.

"Seat yourself, Jackson!" Heidi, the hostess, hollered. *"I'll tell Deb you're here!"*

In typical fashion, Heidi was not manning the hostess podium, even though it was basically her only job. Instead, she was in the bar area off to the right, her arm slung around one the shoulders of one of the clueless guys in town. She spent more time trying to secure a husband than she did trying to earn her paycheck. However, I never said anything. She didn't work for me. She worked for my mother—and Deb didn't seem to mind.

"All right," I answered back, though with less volume.

Harper's wasn't even a third full, so there wasn't a lot of noise that demanded screaming. Heidi simply liked making a spectacle of herself.

I chose a booth in the back of the restaurant, hoping that the dark corner would help me avoid detection from inquisitive townies who had heard about the dead body.

Flipping through the menu was pointless since I had it memorized, but it gave me something to do while I waited. Per usual, I didn't have to flip for long before I saw my mother step up to the end of my table out of the corner of my eye. Closing the menu and laying it down, I folded my hands atop it before turning my attention to her.

"Philly cheesesteak, rings, coleslaw, please," I said, tacking a grin to the end of my statement.

"Coleslaw is a vegetable, I suppose," Deb stared down at me, one eyebrow raised.

For a few moments, we stared at each other.

"And...that's all," I said.

"Anything else you want to tell me about?" Deb asked.

"I might get pecan pie for dessert," I said, casually. "I haven't made my mind up yet. Is there vanilla ice cream to go on top?"

Deb glared down at me, her hands going to her hips.

"If you serve the pie hot and put the ice cream on top, it gets all melty and gooey and so delicious and—"

"You know darn well what I'm getting' at," Deb said. "Don't play the fool."

"I'm not playing. It's genetic," I snipped.

"You want your Philly cheesesteak or a knuckle sandwich?"

"Do you want a tip or a bad review on the internet?"

"Little man," Deb leaned in, her hands digging into her hips, "I can do this all night."

Grandly, I rose in the booth until I was standing in the seat, doing my best to not lose my balance on the springy cushion. I held my arms out wide and addressed the restaurant.

"*Excuse me, please, everyone!*" I announced loudly, looking around at all of the startled diners. "*I found a dead body at a campsite out in Wilford Woods! No. I don't know anything. Yes, I'm one of the suspects they are eliminating from their very short list. Yes. I was with Sawyer. I don't know his thoughts and don't speak for him. You will have to bother him if you want his opinion on things. I—as of now and forever—have none.*"

Then I plopped back down in my seat. Unfortunately, my forehead hit the faux Tiffany style pendant light that hung over the table, sending it swinging. Immediately, I reached up and rubbed my forehead, a scowl coming to my face as I glared up at my mother.

"Happy?" I snapped.

"Graceful," Deb said blandly, reaching out to steady the lamp.

"I want my food."

"I want a son who isn't so contentious."

"Was that on your word-of-the-day calendar?" I asked. "Define it for me. Actually…spell it."

"You're just so special, ain'tcha?" Deb snapped back. "Too darn good for this town and everyone in it!"

Wisely, Deb spun on her heels to go put my order in with the cook, Beau, who also happened to be Sawyer's brother. I didn't have a chance to say something equally rude in response and completely ruin my chance of getting a hot dinner that I didn't have to cook myself. With the disappearance of Deb, I sank back in my seat, wishing my body to be absorbed into the red vinyl cushion. Becoming invisible, or at least developing a chameleon-like quality, would have been my greatest wish at that moment.

I'd shown my entire rear to the restaurant in an effort to get my mother to stop badgering me about the gossip she'd heard through the town prayer chain. Why I'd done it, I wasn't sure, but having to explain my involvement in the appearance of two dead bodies in town in as many months had put me in a dour mood. Three dead bodies, actually if you wanted to get technical about things. Of course, thanks to my historically *contentious* relationship with my mother, I was often dour while dining at Harper's.

One might ask themselves why I had dinner at Harper's at least three times a week if my mother and I had such a rocky relationship. I had no answer for that inquisitive person. Beau Robison knew how to make a superb cheesesteak, though. Deb rarely charged me for my meals, too. In fact, there had been less than a handful of times I'd actually had to pay for my meals when dining at Harper's. That's the silver lining when your mother owns the joint. However, after the scene I'd just made, it was unlikely I was going to get out of that night's meal without paying—and leaving a great tip.

Slipping my phone from my pocket, I buried my nose in an ebook. I actually had a paperback copy of the book on my bedside table at home, but I'd also purchased a digital copy. It's nice to be able to have a good book everywhere you go without having to pack a physical copy. Digital books also provide the added bonus of giving a person an excuse to not be social in public. Not that I had to worry about too many people approaching my table at Harper's. After the scene I'd made, only the heartiest Head Rock Harbor citizen would bother me. And one of those had already taken their turn.

The others were probably at Bernie's Tavern, slipping into an alcoholic stupor or fighting over a bet on a game of pool.

Somehow, I managed to forget my troubles and get so entranced in my book that I didn't notice the restaurant filling up as I sat there, waiting on my food. The cacophony of conversations going on around me was lost to the buzz of the words from the book swishing around in my head. So, when Deb appeared at my tableside and slapped my plate on the table, I jumped, dropping my phone into my lap.

"Here you go, you ingrate," Deb snipped, though her heart wasn't in it.

Two of my onion rings, rattled by the violent dropping of the plate, rolled off and onto the table. They wouldn't have rolled off if the pile of rings hadn't been so massive. The amount of rings provided to me let me know that Deb wasn't actually all that mad.

Without another word, Deb rushed off, obviously to deal with the recent influx of customers waiting to have their orders taken. The crowd had saved me from the ongoing hostility between Deb and I escalating. At least until another day.

I'd barely had time to return the errant onion rings to my cheesesteak meal platter before my phone buzzed in my lap. Bringing my phone up level with the tabletop, I scrolled to my messages. Sawyer had texted me.

How long does this gun powder test result take?

Smiling, I responded: *You worried?*

It took a second of watching the three little dots bouncing on my screen before Sawyer finally responded.

LOL Nah. Not really. Just wondering.

I responded simply: *A few hours to a few days. Not sure how many resources HRHPD has.*

Sawyer responded quickly with a thumbs up emoji.

GSR tests—or pGSR tests—generally take only a few hours or a day to analyze after samples are collected. I wasn't sure how long testing our clothes would take, but the swabs from our hands couldn't take that long. At least not in a city with a decent forensics lab at their disposal. Marv and Deacon had probably sent mine and Sawyer's tests off to the city for analyzing, though. I didn't have a working knowledge of Head Rock Harbor Police Department's forensic abilities. Maybe there was a lab in town where Deacon worked and the samples would be processed quickly.

Either way, my stomach was going to be knotted up until I got the "all clear" notice.

I suddenly wondered, as I reached for the ketchup, if Marv or Deacon would even bother to let Sawyer and me know if our tests came back clear. It was possible they would keep everything tightly under their hats until a prime suspect was identified. That thought only made my stomach knot up tighter. Not wanting to work myself into a loss of appetite, I did my best to push all thoughts of the GSR test out of my brain.

I uncapped and upended the ketchup over my platter and jostled out a healthy dollop to dip my rings into, then recapped the bottle. Returning it to its spot on the table by the inner wall of the booth, I dug into my dinner.

The first onion ring, dipped in ketchup, wasn't even to my lips before a ruckus outside somehow cut through the cacophony in the restaurant. As if controlled by the same string, every head in the restaurant turned to look at the front wall of the joint. Unfortunately, all of the front windows to Harper's Bar & Grill were opaque and multicolored—like stained glass, but less classy—so it was impossible to tell what was going on. The only thing I could make out through the windows was several shadows passing by the windows, created by the headlights of cars pulling up for dinner or drinking.

Shooting a glance across the restaurant, I caught Deb's eye. Immediately, our contentious relationship melted away—if only momentarily—and she nodded at me. I slid from my booth as she told the diners she was waiting on she'd be back. Both of us rushed across the restaurant to the front door, intent on finding out what had caused such a commotion in the parking lot. A few diners slipped away from their tables and followed us, but most of the patrons of Harper's had some level of decorum and stayed in their seats.

When Deb whipped open the front door and the handful of us spilled out onto the front walk of the restaurant, we were greeted by the most creative cursing I'd ever heard. My eyes immediately landed on Mavis Attberry, clad in a long-sleeve plaid flannel and overalls, and work boots that weren't even tied. Her hands were cuffed behind her back and Jeremy was leading her past the front of Harper's towards his department issued car.

Marv's car was parked next to Jeremy's and he was leaned back against the hood, his arms crossed over his chest. Officer Riley was nearby, looking nervous, unsure of how to support his chief or the lead detective.

"What's going on here?" Deb barked as Jeremy led Mavis past the crowd to the back passenger door of his car.

"Get back inside, Deb," Marv said, waving her off. "Police business."

"You're on my property, Marvin Bucksworth!" Deb snapped. "You go out back to the trailer park and arrest one of my tenants? That's my business."

He made a noise like Ebenezer Scrooge and waved her off again. The patrons who had followed us outside were mumbling behind us.

Knowing that hollering at him in front of practically the whole town wasn't going to get me anywhere, I rushed over to Marv. Jeremy was wrestling Mavis into the back of his car with Officer Riley's help, and it looked like Mavis was giving meaning to the term "hazard pay."

"What are you doing, Marv?" I whisper-hissed at him when I came to stand before him as he sat back against the hood of his car. "What did Mavis do?"

Out of the corner of my eye, I saw Deb starting to march over, and I held my hand out to indicate she should stay put. Fortunately, she heeded my request.

Marv grumbled so only I could hear, "Who around here likes playing with shotguns, Jackson?"

I frowned at him for a moment before my eyes grew wide.

"You've got to be kidding me, Marv," I said, shaking my head. "Mavis didn't have anything to do with that body."

"You say." Marv shrugged then spat an imaginary piece of something from between his teeth at the ground. "But she's shot up enough things around here that she needs her hands tested, too."

I tried to give him a look that conveyed how stupid he was being.

"You know this is downright ridiculous, Marv," I said. "It's been too long to do the test anyway. It's been well over eight hours. Even if her test is positive, it proves nothing. And Mavis shoots up doors and vehicles. Maybe the occasional street sign. She's never hurt a person. Unless feelings count."

Marv couldn't help but let a sliver of a smile appear on his face before forcing it away.

"She took a shot at Lardell Simmons a couple years back," Marvin stated matter-of-factly.

"*The back window of his car.*" I groaned. "He wasn't even in the car. He was in his house."

Suddenly stern, he said, "Riley came down here earlier and tried nicely to get her to come to the department. She didn't want to play nice. Here we are. With a warrant."

He started to dig in his breast pocket and I waved him off.

"A warrant doesn't make this any less stupid," I said.

Marv shrugged. "Covering our bases. And this ain't your business anyhow. You're also a suspect. Do you want to spend your time in jail until *your* test comes back?"

"If you want me to own this whole town, you go right ahead," I said, holding my hands out.

Marv gave his Scrooge-like response again and pushed away from his car.

"Marv," I said, "don't do this to her. She won't last the night in jail. You know that."

Though it was unspoken between us, Mavis had a considerable drinking problem. She was an alcoholic, through and through. A night in a cell without a drink would be catastrophic for her. It wasn't an exaggeration to say that her health would be in danger if she had to spend that long without alcohol. When you also considered that Mavis didn't do well around other people, especially loud ones in neighboring cells, jail would be the end of her.

"We're bringing her right back after we get our samples," he said, not looking at me as he rounded his car to jump inside. "Everybody in this town is so dramatic."

I contemplated kicking his fender as he slammed his door, but decided that doing so was actually an arrestable offense. Fortunately, my brain delayed the signal to my foot before I was in my own pair of cuffs.

Mavis Attberry, the town drunk—or one of the most infamous ones—and shotgun enthusiast, had shot up plenty of things in her time. Harming another human being physically? Rarely if ever. She'd certainly never *shot* another person. Damaged property? Hurt feelings? Ruined town events? Terrified Tourists? Well…yes. But no actual harm was ever done by her to anyone.

As Marv backed out, blinding me with his headlights, I glanced over at Jeremy's car. Officer Riley and Jeremy had finally wrangled Mavis into the backseat. She was sitting there, defeated and glum, her face pressed to the glass. She was facing the opposite direction, so I couldn't see if she was making faces or not, but she looked deflated.

"Jeremy!" I called out. "What are you doing?"

Jeremy, startled by the sound, whipped around, his eyes searching the crowd that was growing outside of Harper's now. When his eyes landed on me, they turned to slits.

"You're not a detective, Jackson!" he hollered back. "Go spend time between the pages with Agatha Christie!"

I glowered at him and I could tell from the flash of worry on his face that he knew he'd gone too far.

"You're not much of one either if you're going along with this!" I snapped back. "And Marv's a fool if he thinks this is a good use of taxpayers' money!"

Jeremy winced as the group behind me broke into whispers and chuckles.

After a moment of shame and embarrassment, he glowered at me, but he didn't respond in kind. Instead, he continued to glare at me as he opened the driver door of his car, slipped into the seat, and slammed the door. Seconds later, he was backing out of the lot as well. Officer Riley, catching my eyes, gave me an apologetic shrug, then dashed off towards his cruiser.

I wanted to pick up a rock and throw it at Jeremy's back window. Again, I considered the legalities of such an act and if I would survive a night in the pokey. I settled for standing there and glaring at him as he drove away.

"*Idiots!*" I hollered as Jeremy's car and Riley's cruiser made their way down the road away from Harper's.

When I finally turned around, everyone but Deb had sauntered back into the restaurant. My shoulders slumped and I shook my head as I shuffled back to the front door. As I passed my mother, she grabbed my forearm and looked at me.

"You're too darn special, but you're a good kid," she said.

"Mavis didn't do anything," I said. "Well, nothing to do with that body."

"I know she didn't," Deb said. "She's a hellraiser, but she's decent people. I told her a long time ago she didn't have to pay a lot fee as long as she lived here. God knows she's living on a budget. But I still get six-fifty from her every month. Just like every other tenant. It's always cash, but I don't ask questions."

"She's good people," I parroted, nodding.

Deb examined my face for a moment.

"Dinner's on me," Deb said.

"Isn't it always?" I managed a chuckle.

"And so's dessert," she added.

She hooked a hand around the back of my neck and pulled me down to kiss the side of my head. Before I could react, she had pulled away and slipped into Harper's once again. I stood there for a moment, considering the day's events. When it occurred to me that my dinner was likely getting cold, I made my way back inside. I didn't know if I still had the appetite for dinner and dessert, but since it was free, I'd do my best. Like a good Midwestern boy would.

Chapter Five

Waking the next morning to a curt text from Marv that my GSR test had come back negative from the lab in Dubuque should have put me in a good mood. I was glad Deacon had gotten my test into the lab quickly. Even though I knew I hadn't killed the man at the campsite, I would have been nervous until the results were actually returned. Now, my body could stop contemplating a bout of diarrhea, and Marv and the rest of the police department would know I was in the clear.

Before I got ready for the day with a shower and breakfast upstairs, I shot off a text to Sawyer to see if he got his results. It wasn't until I was showered, clothed, coiffed, and sitting down to eggs and toast in my kitchenette that he responded. Sawyer was also in the clear. Of course, I had no reason to suspect Sawyer of murdering the man, and I knew he was incapable of such a thing, but I was still worried for him.

I'm typically a logical, level-headed kind of guy. I own and operate a bookstore, write best-selling detective novels under a pen name, and mind my business. I don't do drugs.

I don't drink heavily—*usually*—and I get plenty of sunshine and exercise. However, like most red-blooded Americans, I don't necessarily always trust our government. From the local elected mayor up to the President of the United States, I'm skeptical.

One little mistake in a lab result and an innocent man can easily go to jail for life. It's not like it hasn't happened before.

Fortunately, that wasn't going to be the case for Sawyer or me.

Head Rock Harbor Books opened at nine o'clock and the first part of my morning was filled with townie regulars. The romance, young adult, and horror enthusiasts were out in full force. With only my regulars to occupy my time, however, I spent a good portion of the morning dusting and then tapping away at my laptop in between customers.

Though I try to not make it a habit to write my *Detective Randy Melton Mystery series* while the store is open, it has been done. With so few customers and not much work to be done in the clean and organized store, it felt wasteful to not do something productive. So, I'd brought my laptop down to the check-out counter and tried to get a few hundred words in before lunch.

No one but my agent, editor, and publisher in New York was aware, but I was the writer behind a wildly popular and best-selling mystery series. To be honest, the whole thing had been a fluke. Right after college, I'd submitted a manuscript I'd worked on for all four years of my undergraduate program. A boutique agency signed me to a contract—which included an advance that was so paltry it was laughable—and we got to work editing.

Somehow, my editor convinced an acquisitions editor at a major publishing house to give the manuscript a look, and the next thing I knew, I was a published author. Using a pen name to write my *Detective Randy Melton Mystery series* had been a choice I'd made when I thought no one would care about the book. When it turned out that a lot of people actually cared, the choice had been a boon.

The promotion and advertising campaign set into action by the publisher had been the catalyst. Starting small, books were offered as advance copies through the typical channels, and special advance copies were sent to influencers in all of the reader communities on all the social media sites. One influencer loving the book turned into dozens loving the book, which turned into Harrison Garner—my pen name— becoming a best-selling author overnight.

And that's when I started to have panic attacks.

I couldn't sleep. I couldn't eat. I was afraid to leave the bookstore. The thought of having to do podcasts or internet-based talk shows or give interviews to magazines paralyzed me. Before my agency or publisher could even think to ask about a second book in the series, I had decided I would never write again.

Apparently, concerned about the loss of revenue a sequel to a best-selling book would generate, my agency and publisher agreed that Harrison Garner could be elusive. If I kept writing and fulfilled my future contractual obligations, they would never tell people the true identity of Harrison Garner. As big a mystery as every murder Detective Randy Melton solved, the intrigue of no one knowing the true identity of Harrison Garner made fans even more rabid. Influencers ate it up, doing whole series on their channels about trying to unravel the mystery of who Harrison Garner could be.

Many people speculated that Harrison Garner was an established best-selling author pulling a fast one on readers. Other people heavily implied that Harrison Garner was an influential politician—or even a royal! It was ridiculous.

However, I could finally sleep, eat, and leave the store. I didn't have to worry about being a public figure. I simply turned in my contractually obligated pages, cashed my royalty checks, and kept my mouth shut. With the bookstore bringing in enough money to cover my bills and expenses, I had more money than was reasonable for a single guy living in an efficiency apartment over a bookstore.

I tried to not let it bother me. We all have our crosses to bear.

That morning, at the check-out counter, "Harrison Garner" was contemplating changing the physicality of the villain in his sixth novel. Maybe he needed to be a tall handsome blond with curly hair, a badge, and an attitude. Or maybe a smalltown police chief who didn't know his butt from a hole in the ground. However, the more I played with ideas, the guiltier I felt.

"Crap," I muttered to no one as I saved the Word document and closed my laptop.

"*Mew.*" Rattlesnatches looked up at me from his lounging spot on the counter a few feet away.

"I know," I said. "I'm a turd."

My cat blinked at me and laid his head down. I don't know if that was him agreeing or dismissing my wildly hurtful and inaccurate claim. Sometimes Rattlesnatches is vague.

A glance at the clock told me that there was still a half hour until lunch. Since the store hadn't had any visitors in the last thirty minutes, I decided an extended lunch wasn't unreasonable. So, I made sure the register was locked up, gave Rattlesnatches the talk about staying out of trouble, hit the lights, grabbed my keys and a light jacket, and headed out of the store. Giving the knob a jiggle from outside, I was satisfied that things would be fine until I got back.

Though I knew my choice was the correct one, I still found myself kicking at the pavement with the toes of my sneakers as I walked the few blocks to the police department. Trying to make Jeremy and Marv the villain in my next book made me confront some hard truths. The hardest one being that I had acted petulantly and reacted immaturely to them taking Mavis into the police department for a GSR test.

Jeremy and Marv were simply doing their jobs. A man was dead. He deserved justice if he had been murdered. That was more important than how I felt or Mavis' dislike for authority. Having essentially humiliated both the chief and the town detective in front of Harper's clientele had been a huge gaffe on my part. However, facts were facts. Intentional or not, I'd been a world-class jerk to two guys I respected— one of whom I considered my best friend.

Apologizing was the right thing to do, even if the words tasted like crud coming up.

When I swung the metal and glass door of the police department open and stepped into the lobby, I was greeted by a gust of icy air. Even in early April, Marv had the air conditioning on to mitigate the suffering Gloria dealt with as she went through the change of life. Even if she was the 911 dispatcher and not in charge, the guys liked to keep her happy. It was easier for them to put on a coat and a hat than it was to tell her to strip off a few layers.

One option was acceptable. The other was a lawsuit.

I let the door swing shut behind me and glanced around the small lobby. Gloria's voice carried down the long hallway from Dispatch at the left end of the building. Without listening too closely, I could tell she was exchanging a recipe with someone. Head Rock Harbor's never had a lot of 911 situations, so Gloria has one of the cushiest jobs in town.

Officer Ashley Riley was stationed at a desk in the corner, his back turned to me, hunched over a computer, tapping away at the keys. Writing a report, obviously, Officer Riley had apparently never taken a typing class in his life. Index fingers were his only tools as he strained and struggled to complete his task.

"Ashley," I said, causing him to jerk and spin in his chair, "are Marv and Germ here?"

Ashley, wide-eyed at my sudden appearance, merely nodded.

"I need to talk to them if—"

"They're in the interview room," he said, hooking a thumb towards the hall. "They've been in there for a bit."

"Okay," I said. "Thanks."

"Well, they're busy, and—" Ashley began as I turned on my heels and headed down the hallway.

Though I wasn't intentionally ignoring what Ashley had to say, I knew that if I didn't apologize immediately, I never would. Then Germ and Marv would be mad at me forever and it would be a long time before we all were back to normal. Besides, whatever they were doing in the interview room couldn't be that important. Head Rock Harbor Police Department wasn't trying to infiltrate the mob, the international cartel, or plan huge drug busts.

Interrupting them for one minute could not be that devastating.

When I got halfway down the hall and approached the door on the right side with the placard which read "Interview Room"—I rapped my knuckles on the door lightly. Voices inside penetrated the thin door, but I couldn't quite make out the words in the discussion. However, I hadn't come to the PD to eavesdrop, so it didn't matter. When I knocked, the voices died off.

After a few seconds, and getting no response, I lifted my fist to knock once more, but the door suddenly opened. Jeremy frowned at me and stepped out into the hall, forcing me to move out of the way to make room for him. Before he could close the door to the Interview Room, I had a moment to be nosy and glance inside. Marv was sitting on one side of the long wooden table and four others were sitting on the other. When he saw me, he gave me a frown and a shake of his head. Somehow, he also managed to look amused. Then the door was closed.

"What are you doing here, Jacks?" Jeremy pulled my attention away from the room.

Shaking my head to clear my thoughts, I turned to look at him.

"Sorry to interrupt…whatever is going on," I gestured at the door. "But I had to come down here to talk to you. If I didn't, I'd be thinking about it all day."

Jeremy looked concerned.

"Did you think of something about the body?" he asked, reaching for his pocket.

"No, no, no," I said, waving him off.

His arm fell back to his side. I heaved a sigh and slumped.

"I was rude to you and Marv last night," I said, mumbling down at my chest. "I wanted to come apologize."

The corner of Jeremy's mouth turned up.

"I'm sorry," I said, looking up at him. "Okay?"

"That could have been a text," he said, teasing.

"Apologies are best in person," I said. "Forgive me?"

Jeremy nodded. "It's all right, Jacks. I get it. I know how you feel about Mavis. She got home safely an hour after we picked her up. I made sure of it. Okay?"

"Okay."

"She described things I could do to myself as I let her out of the car—in horrifyingly graphic detail—but she got home in the same condition we found her in."

I chuckled.

"All right," I said. "Again, I'm sorry. I shouldn't have let my mouth get away from me. I could have chewed you out privately."

Jeremy grinned. "Like, over a homemade dinner on a Monday evening? Because you feel so bad and all, of course?"

Rolling my eyes, I said, "Fine. Yeah. I can make dinner for you as my penance."

"It's the very least you could do, I feel," he said, crossing his arms over his broad chest.

"Don't push it, Sass-quatch."

Jeremy gave a full-throated laugh and dropped his arms.

"Seven?" I asked.

"Sure," Jeremy agreed. "Seven's good."

"Will you tell Marv I'm sorry?" I asked. "If he requires an in-person apology, I can come back later. He looks busy."

I glanced at the door.

Jeremy moved to block the door, as though I had x-ray vision.

"Jeez," I said. "Calm down."

"You're not a detective, Jacks," he shook his head, amused. "Keep your nose out of police business for once."

I huffed.

"I never put my nose in police business," I stammered. "Police business sticks itself in my nose. *Once.* Stop being so dramatic."

I turned to walk away, but Jeremy's hand shot out and he grabbed my forearm. Turning, I looked down at his hand, then up at him. Jeremy's eyes locked on mine, then he glanced down at his hand before quickly releasing my forearm.

"I don't want you to get hurt," he said quietly. "Okay?"

"I won't get—"

"Next time I might not be quick enough to keep a psychopath from stabbing you," Jeremy said, his voice thick with some emotion. "And I would never forgive myself. Do you hear me, Jacks? I hope you're listening."

We stared into each other's eyes for a moment and, finally, I merely nodded. For some reason, my chest felt tight. My throat felt like the Sahara.

"Like the NSA," I said.

Jeremy cocked his head to the side.

"Always listening," I shrugged.

"That's how you end up in trouble," he said, grinning.

I ignored him. "Is that the Nelson family in there?"

Jeremy's head fell back and he looked up at the ceiling.

"Mason, Nelson, Kenny, Myr—"

Before I could finish saying Myrna's name, Jeremy had grabbed ahold of me again. This time by the shoulders. He spun me around and started leading me down the hall to the lobby. Over my protestations, he pushed me towards the front door and swung it open. Before I could stop him, he had deposited me on the front stoop of the PD and blocked the doorway with his body, looming over me.

"Is Marv breaking the news to them?" I was unfazed. "Because I bet they already—"

"Stop it," Jeremy said firmly, but gently. "You're done."

"Jeez," I said. "I didn't ask to inspect the evidence. Just asking if he's telling the family that their relative is dead."

For the longest of minutes, Jeremy stared at me from the doorway of the PD, and by the time the minute had passed, I had melted. It was impossible to see the look of worry and concern in his eyes as he considered me without feeling guilty.

"Seven o'clock?" he finally asked. "I'm in the mood for pasta. Some garlic bread. How about you?"

"Pasta works," I agreed, nodding, looking down at my shoes.

Jeremy reached out and bopped me under the chin so I was forced to look up at him.

"Keep yourself safe, Jacks," he said warmly. "Stay out of danger. Okay?"

"Yeah. Okay."

He started to turn to close the door, but then he was facing me once more.

"And stay away from Sawyer."

I snorted. "His GSR test was negative, too. He texted me about it this morning."

If Jeremy thought Sawyer was dangerous, he was out of his mind.

"I said what I said," Jeremy replied. "Stay away from him."

Then he swung the door shut and I was left out in the April air that was somehow warmer than the air in the police department. Frowning, I stared blankly and unfocused at the door as I considered Jeremy's comments.

"You're not the boss of me," I mumbled petulantly at the door, kicking at the concrete with the toe of my shoe.

Since it was obvious that my services were not only not required, but not welcome, at the Head Rock Harbor Police Department, I headed back to the store. As I walked, taking my time since I had an extended lunch, I thought about what Jeremy had said. Had he uncovered something about Sawyer that he wouldn't—*or couldn't*—share with me? Did I need to be cautious around Sawyer? Was I already in danger and simply didn't know it yet?

Something in my gut told me the truth. Sawyer was no more a physical danger to me than my own mother. Jeremy had other reasons for his command. But my mind wouldn't let me confront that reality. That thing that fluttered in my gut was unspeakable. So, I pushed it away.

Instead, I thought about the Nelson family in the Interview Room with Marv and Jeremy. None of them had turned to look when Jeremy had opened the door, but I had recognized them anyway. They were hard not to recognize at a glance. Was Marv merely breaking the news to them about their dead relative—if the guy who had "Nelson" etched inside his cooler really was their family—or was it something else?

Of course, Ashley had said that Jeremy and Marv had been in the Interview Room for "a bit." Simply breaking bad news to a family doesn't take all that long. Sure, you have to provide comfort and empathy to people who have lost a family member, but that doesn't take all that long. Usually, families want to go home and grieve together. They don't want to share those moments with a police chief and a detective.

When I really put my mind to it, the police didn't call people down to the station to break news about a dead family member. They came to your home. Especially in a small town where everyone knew everyone else. If Marv had called in the Nelsons to talk about the dead body, it was more than simply informing them of his death.

He had questions for them.

And I desperately wanted to know those questions.

Jeremy was right. My nose didn't know how to mind its business.

Chapter Six

How about I buy you lunch tomorrow when you close up at noon?

Staring down at the latest message from Jeremy as I sat at the kitchenette table in my apartment, steam was still rising from the giant casserole dish full of Taco Pasta Bake. The sliced French loaf was oozing garlicy, buttery goodness into the pan next to it. I'd cooked for forty-five minutes after closing up the shop for the day at six, only to have Jeremy cancel on me at the last minute. The sight and smell of the food was making my stomach grumble ravenously.

It better be a good lunch.

The response was meant to be snippy, though I wasn't truly angry. Germ had explained that work had gotten in the way of our plans to have dinner together—and I couldn't begrudge him his work. Paying bills is more important than eating pasta, if only barely.

When Jeremy responded with a laughing emoji and a promise to buy me a nice lunch on Tuesday, I set my phone down next to my plate.

Since I was no longer waiting for him to show up before eating, propriety went out the window. I scooped a square of the pasta onto my plate and deposited two slices of garlic bread next to it. Seconds later, I was devouring the dinner I'd worked hard to prepare for the two of us. As I silently ate in the small kitchenette, Rattlesnatches sprawled out on my bed on the other side of my apartment, dozing lazily.

Though the food was delicious, it didn't feel satisfying. Probably because I'd expected to have Jeremy across the table from me—someone to talk to and share my day with over a meal. Eating alone had never really bothered me before. In fact, when I went out to eat in town at any of the local joints, I usually went alone. However, sitting alone in my apartment felt lonely.

That might have been why I went out to eat so often.

Then again, it occurred to me that it might not be the lack of company that was bothering me. If I was to be completely honest with myself, I had wanted Jeremy across the table from me so I could sleuth some details about the dead body out of him. Or, at least, I'd *also* wanted to sleuth out some details about the case from him.

Jeremy isn't stupid. There was no way I could trick him into simply dropping information about the case. However, if I was persistent, it was possible he'd give me a few nuggets of information to placate me. With a few extra details, I'd have a chance of piecing things together and could probably figure out the path of their investigation going forward. I didn't need much. A few crumbs thrown my way out of pity or annoyance. That was all.

Putting my nose in police business wasn't exactly wise or appreciated—and I knew it would be the first thing Jeremy would point out if I tried to get information from him. After Prescott Pemberton's murder in the harbor at the beginning of Spring, Jeremy was convinced I considered myself the Jessica Fletcher of East Central Iowa. The thing was—I'd gotten pulled into Prescott's death investigation accidentally. Being asked to assess the man's belongings for auction and communicate with his sister across the country dragged me into the mess.

It hadn't been intentional.

Not really.

I couldn't help that I had also found the crashed car and body of his assistant—and co-conspirator of his murder—during the course of the investigation. Sometimes I simply stumbled upon trouble. My chest suddenly swelled with indignation. Jeremy had quickly forgotten the fact that I'd actually solved Prescott's and his assistant's murders. If it hadn't been for me, it was possible Jeremy could have been the next victim. And a murderer would have been on the loose, never to face justice.

Yeah. I thought to myself. *He doesn't appreciate me at all.*

I finished my dinner, and took my plate and fork to the sink.

That was the thing about Head Rock Harbor. Everyone was in everyone's business all of the time. When you live in a small community of less than five thousand people, it's hard not to know everyone. People gossip because there's not much going on. When something is going on, they gossip even harder. I knew for a fact that I wasn't the only person in town thinking about the dead body in the woods and what had happened. I was simply the most vocal about it when Jeremy and Marv were around.

If being open with my thoughts is a crime, lock me up!

Once my plate and the fork were washed, dried, and put away, I returned to the table to cover the casserole dish and garlic bread and stow them in the fridge. I'd barely put my hand to the roll of tin foil when I was stopped by a thought. How quickly and naturally it had come to me was concerning, but I was also intrigued with my own cleverness.

Before I could overthink things, I took the serving spoon and nudged the pasta around in the casserole until it was in an even layer. I made it look pretty, as though no one had touched it. Then I took a length of tin foil and wrapped up the remaining garlic bread, organizing it was beautifully as possible in the silver sheet. I covered the casserole with another piece of the foil, placed the garlic bread package on top, and scooped up the casserole dish.

Minutes later, I had walked halfway across town, one arm cradling the casserole dish and garlic bread while the other knocked on a door.

The Nelsons were what other people in town might label "rednecks." They liked to hunt, fish, shoot, go fishing, wear Carhartt and overalls, work boots, and ball caps announcing their favorite beers. They drove four-wheelers recklessly on the outskirts of town and through land that often didn't belong to them. They drank, they cursed, and they were more often than not behind the biggest brawls that broke out at Bernie's Tavern when a game was on the T.V.

They were raising hell when God was still best friends with Lucifer, Deb always said.

For all their ways, they lived in one of the prettier, more affluent neighborhoods in Head Rock Harbor. Walking up the concrete path that led through the well-manicured lawn to the faux-Tudor style home, one would never think *hellraisers*. When one of the Nelsons answered the door, though, it was easy to wonder if you had knocked on the wrong door.

Myrna Nelson, the matriarch and put-upon ringleader of the clan, answered the door in her nightgown. The green cotton dress was covered in embroidered daisies, had a scooped neck, had leg of mutton sleeves, and barely came down to her knees. A mismatched silk bonnet in a burnt orange hung perilously to the bulb of hair on her head, and a half-smoked cigarette dangled from between her lips. I couldn't tell if she had been in the process of removing her make up or it had simply given up for the day.

"What do you want?" she hacked.

An earthy, musty smell was emanating from Myrna Nelson, and it wasn't cigarettes or incense.

"Mrs. Nelson?" I did my best to smile sympathetically, "You might not remember me, but—"

"Jackson Harper," she said with a nod.

Myrna Nelson leaned until she was propped against the doorjamb and crossed her arms over her ample chest as she stared at me blandly.

"I done told you none of my boys had anything to do with that flat tire of yours," she said. "I ain't payin' for nothin'."

Frowning, I was immediately confused by what Mrs. Nelson had said as a form of greeting. I'd never had a flat tire that I'd blamed on one of the Nelson boys. I'd never asked the Nelsons for money. However, Myrna had gotten my name right, so I couldn't help but wonder if I hadn't gone crazy and forgotten an event like a flat tire.

One more look at Myrna's make up and I realized I was not the crazy one.

"Jackson Harper," I agreed. "But you've mistaken me for someone else. I…never had a flat tire. Or blamed one of your boys for one."

She eyed me suspiciously for a moment.

It occurred to me then that Myrna Nelson had made a mistake—but maybe I was making one that was worse. What if the dead guy wasn't even related to the Nelsons? What if, after talking to the Nelsons, Marv found out that the dead guy simply had the same last name. Nelson was an incredibly common last name. It wasn't unreasonable to think that the dead man had no affiliations with anyone in town—even ones with the same, common, last name.

You're standing here with a casserole, Jackson. How else are you going to explain it?

"All right then," Myrna said. "Sorry. People in this town are always accusing my boys of somethin'. I get y'all mixed up sometimes."

I answered her non-apology with a smile.

"I heard about your relative," I said slowly. "I thought a casserole might be needed."

Myrna clicked her tongue and slumped against the doorframe.

"Oh, lord," she said. "who'da thought I'd outlive Carter? I guess he had to kill himself to beat me to the grave. I got one foot in it already."

She pulled the cigarette from her mouth and hacked into her elbow dramatically. Looking at Myrna Nelson, even someone who didn't know her would place her in her mid-50s. And that would be accurate. Smoker or not, she didn't look like she was on the dock of the River Styx. Regardless of how she felt about her health, one thing was clear. I hadn't made a mistake.

Carter Nelson. I had a name.

Of course, now that the family had been notified, I probably would've found out as much in the newspaper the following morning.

You're super slick, Jackson.

However, it would have taken at least thirty minutes over dinner to get that much out of Jeremy. Maybe it was a win after all.

"I was sorry to hear about your loss," I said, gesturing to the casserole in my arm. "I know it's not much, but I thought it might help a bit during this difficult time."

"Well," Myrna asked, reaching for the casserole, "what is it?"

"It's," I began as Myrna jerked it from my arm, "Taco Pasta Bake. Cheesy, meaty pasta. Some garlic bread. It's nothing fancy, but it's delicious."

Myrna gave a hacking laugh as she pulled up a corner of the foil to look into the dish.

"We don't do fancy around here, anyway," she said. "This looks good. Thank you, Jackson. This is mighty fine of you."

Again, I replied with a smile.

"I'm really sorry to hear about Carter," I said. "I don't know if you know this, but Sawyer and I were the ones who found him out there. I feel horrible for your family."

"Marv told me two of the boys here in town found him," Myrna appraised me. "He hadn't said who. But I guess I owe you thanks for making sure he didn't stay out there to rot. Of course, I'm sure Colton would have found him in a day or two."

My stomach turned at the thought of finding a rotted and decomposing Carter Nelson. The gunshot wound had been enough.

"Colton?" I asked.

"His son," Myrna took her cigarette and flicked it over my shoulder into the yard. I'd had to fight the urge to duck. Fortunately, Myrna was an expert cigarette flicker. "My nephew. Him and Carter been up here from Burlington to do some fishing and camping."

I stared at Myrna for a moment, considering how to best ask my next question without offending her and getting the door slammed in my face.

"I guess Colton got tired of being out at the campsite," I said simply.

She shook her head, amused. "He gets up here and he just has to go off running with my boys—his cousins. The four of them...well, camping and fishing with his daddy didn't seem nearly as exciting once he got here, you know? Not that I can blame him. Who wants to spend time with their daddy when they can be out actin' a fool with their cousins?"

I chuckled at that.

"Makes sense," I said. "Well, at least he would have eventually returned to the campsite when it was time to pack up and go home."

Myrna nodded.

"How...how old is Colton?"

Myrna stared at me for a moment, suddenly caught my drift, and waved me off.

"He's twenty-five, darlin'," she said. "I say *boy*, but he's 'bout the same age as mine."

"Oh," I said. "Good. Well, I mean, I'd hate to think of a younger boy finding his father like that."

Myrna's face softened at my sentiment.

"Just a waste," she said, simply.

"Well," I said neutrally, "the circumstances are unfortunate."

"You ain't lyin'," Myrna was shaking her head again. "That old fool."

Her eyes began to glaze as she stared past me, seeing nothing.

"I don't know why he went and done that to hisself," she gave her head a final, violent shake.

As I listened to Myrna talk, it occurred to me that what I'd done was quite possibly the trashiest thing possible. I'd brought a casserole I'd already taken part in to her house in order to get information about her dead relative. Because...*because I was nosy.* This woman had lost her brother, a son had lost his father, and the three Nelson boys had lost an uncle, and I simply couldn't mind my business. She was looking to grieve. I was looking to gossip.

Jeremy's voice in my head, reminding me that I wasn't a detective echoed. Deb's voice always reminding me to mind my own business jointed it. My own conscience telling me what a piece of crap I was rounded out the trio. Obviously, I had taken no time to consider what it would mean to come to this poor woman's house and make her talk about her brother's obvious suicide. What torture was I putting her through simply because I couldn't mind my business?

Of course, there was that voice in the back of my head reminding me that Marv had been in the Interview Room with the Nelsons for "a bit." Longer than it would take to simply tell someone a relative was dead. Marv had also brought them all down to the station to find out the news. He hadn't simply come to her home, like I had, and had a civil, sympathetic, sit-down conversation about finding her brother. It was possible something was fishy—and Marv and Jeremy knew it.

I pushed that voice away. The Nelsons were known hellraisers. Marv had probably thought having them at the station was the most controlled environment to deliver such horrible news. Who knew how Myrna or her "boys" would react. And I didn't know Colton. Maybe he was the ringleader of the hellraisers. It was possible that I would have felt safer delivering such news at the police department, too.

"—but I guess that's what you get for living like he did," Myrna's voice cut through the noise in my head.

I had no idea what she'd been talking about for the last minute or two, but fortunately, it didn't seem that she realized I'd drifted off mentally.

"I suppose so," I said neutrally. "It sure is an awful loss, though."

Myrna grinned, what was probably for her, a million-dollar grin. She jerked from the doorframe as if she'd suddenly realized something.

"I'm so sorry, darlin'," she said. "I haven't even invited you in. You wanna come in and sit for a while?"

I held my hands up with a smile.

"I don't want to impose," I said. "I wanted to pay my condolences and bring the casserole. You should get back to your family."

Again, that smile flashed on Myrna's face. She jiggled the casserole where it was cradled in the crook of her arm.

"Well, I certainly appreciate it. Thank you, Jackson."

"You're welcome," I said. "If you need anything, I'm always down at the bookstore."

We said our "goodbyes" and Myrna went back inside of her house, trying to cradle the casserole in one arm while digging for her cigarettes in her house dress pocket with her other hand. As I walked back down the concrete path from her front porch to the road, my dinner felt sour in my stomach.

I definitely wasn't East Central Iowa's Jessica Fletcher. That lady had class.

I was something that rhymed with it.

Chapter Seven

Tuesday morning at the bookshop was typical, though most days I didn't start out with hating myself. I'd slept fitfully Monday night after leaving Myrna Nelson's house. I'd tossed and turned, sat up for a while and tried to read to make myself sleepy. I watched an episode of an old detective T.V. show on a streaming service. Sleep evaded me.

I tried writing more words in the newest *Detective Randy Melton Mystery series*, but I kept thinking about making the villain a bean pole bookstore owner with curly brown hair and olive skin. Maybe he murdered people by bashing their heads in with thick tomes direct from the shelves of his bookstore? At the very least, his victims got their feelings hurt.

After a few hours of sulking at the check-out counter, I pulled myself out of my bad mood. I'd done a dreadful thing, going to Myrna Nelson's home. However, I was determined to never do something so vile ever again. Even if I had a casserole that wasn't missing a portion to deliver when I did it. I was going to keep my nose in my own business.

I wasn't going to play detective.

Everyone can be a bad person or do a bad thing, but what matters is what you do to fix the mistake you made. As far as Myrna knew, I was showing up simply out of sympathy. And she got a free dinner for her and the boys. She hadn't been hurt by my actions. Only I knew how horrible of a person I was. I had to live with that, and make sure I never did it again. If I was willing to do that, then I had to forgive myself.

Business was slower than usual, but Tuesdays and Wednesdays were never my busiest days. Most everyone knew I was only open until lunch on those days, and unless there was an event in town, or something that drew tourists in, things were slow. I didn't really mind. It gave me two business days to do extra cleaning, organizing, and inventory if needed. It also gave me time to write more words.

So, I spent the second half of the morning responding to an email to my agent and publisher, updating them on my manuscript progress. Then I set about writing, tapping away at my laptop, doing my best to not self-insert myself into the villain. It was slow going at first, but as lunch drew near, the world had melted away and my fingers were flying across the keys at record speed.

It wasn't until a customer knocked on the counter that I jerked to attention and my glazed eyes shot up to see who had interrupted me.

"Is that the new Harrison Garner?"

I stared at the young woman with gritty eyes that hadn't blinked enough in the last hour, trying to focus. When what she said finally registered with my brain, I nervously slapped my laptop shut and reached up to rub my eyes.

"I'm sorry?" I stammered.

"The new Harrison Garner?" she asked.

"What...I mean..."

The young woman grinned at my obvious confusion and jabbed a thumb at the display of books set to the side of the register. A stack of six books, the latest in the Detective Randy Melton series, were proudly and prominently displayed for customers. I'd forgotten. I turned my attention back to the woman, trying to place her. After a moment, I realized she was the young woman who worked at the Casey's convenience store out on the highway coming into town. Or going out of town. Depends on how you looked at it.

"Oh," I said, "yeah. Sorry. That's the fifth book. It's the latest."

"Fifth?" She gasped. "He's put out two more?"

"Five so far. He's working on a sixth from what I hear."

"Do you have the fourth one?" she asked desperately. "I've gotten behind and I don't want to skip around. I know they're essentially standalone mysteries and you don't *have* to read them in order, but you know, I think Randy's relationship with his partner might be getting romantic, and I don't want to miss any of that, so I—"

I laughed. "Yeah. I read them, too. You definitely don't want to miss that."

She smiled.

I pointed a finger. "Mystery section under Garner. The fourth one is titled *An Historical Homicide*. It's set in a museum."

The young woman—*Kelly, I remembered suddenly*—squealed and dashed away.

"Do you want the fifth book, too?" I hollered after her.

"*Yes, please!*" she squealed back, excited to be on a book-finding adventure.

Those were my favorite types of customers. The ones who got excited about books. The ones who treated bookstores like theme parks. I smiled to myself as I pulled one of the books off the stack by the register and set it on the counter for Kelly. When she returned with the fourth book in hand, I rang her up, bagged her books, and made a bit of small talk with her about the series. Then she was on her way, waving and smiling as she left the store.

When she stepped out of the store, as though she'd forgotten that the whole front was lined with windows, she hugged her bag to her chest. Then she took off, practically skipping away. I didn't really know Kelly, never really had an opportunity to interact with her much before, but I decided I liked her. I also grinned at the thought that she'd had a discussion with the author of a book series she loved and would never know it.

A thought occurred to me and I anxiously opened my laptop again. Fortunately, I hadn't ruined anything by suddenly closing it while writing. Everything I'd written was still on the screen and, undeleted by my carelessness. I went to my Word settings to make sure auto-save was on, clicked the save button five times to be sure, then locked my laptop and closed it again.

The dinging of my phone drew my attention from my laptop and I opened it to find a message from Jeremy.

Munchies for lunch?

The upper left-hand corner of my phone told me that lunch was actually in ten minutes, so I shot off a quick response to the affirmative.

Within five minutes, I had the check-out counter organized, the register locked up, and the lights off. Rattlesnatches brushed up against my shins as I made my way to the front door, mewling preciously. I took a minute to give him a couple pets and scratches before explaining that I'd be back for more scratches and pets later. Right at noon, I left the bookstore, locking up behind myself, and headed down the street to Munchies.

The bookstore and Munchies both being located on Harbor Street made it my favorite lunchtime spot. Of course, location wasn't the only positive to Munchies. The food—for what it was—was exceptional. Lardell Simmons, the owner and cook, could make a mean pork tenderloin sandwich. And he made the best coleslaw for miles around. His daughter, Shirley Templeton, was the best waitress outside of a fine-dining establishment.

Though the décor left something to be desired—unless you liked Grandma's Basement Rec Room Chic—it didn't really matter. It was the food that mattered. In my opinion, the jankier the décor at a restaurant, the better the food. It was always the hole-in-the-wall places that paid more attention to cleanliness and deliciousness than they did to trends were always the gems. Munchies definitely fit my theory.

Upon entering the restaurant, Shirley gave me a smile and a wave from behind the counter where she was ringing up a customer. Then she jerked a thumb to the back of the restaurant—not that it was that big of a place. Jeremy was already seated at the booth in the very back, facing the entrance. Something about cops makes them want their back to a wall and to have a clear view of all the entrances.

I guess when you deal with criminals and guns all day, it makes you paranoid. Jauntily, I made my way over to the booth and slid in across from Jeremy, all smiles. Even though I'd started my day out with a nice dose of self-hatred, I was going to get a free lunch from one of my favorite restaurants. What was there to be sour about, after all?

"You're looking chipper," Jeremy said.

"Free lunch," I replied.

"That'll do it."

I didn't bother picking up a menu. My order was always the same at Munchies. Pork tenderloin sandwich, fries with Ranch for dipping, and coleslaw. My mouth was already watering thinking about it. Even the old wood paneling lining the walls couldn't turn me off of my appetite.

"Carter Nelson," Jeremy said suddenly.

Startled, I replied, "What?"

"The guy. In the woods. That you found?" Jeremy's eyebrow rose. "His name is Carter Nelson. He's related to the Nelsons here in town. Like you suggested to Marv."

"Oh."

Jeremy stared at me, his hands folded atop the table.

"You don't have to tell me anything," I said, waving him off with a forced chuckle.

"But I want to, Jacks. We're besties."

Jeremy had an indecipherable look on his face.

"You were right," I said, hoping to wiggle my way out of the obvious conundrum I'd created by visiting Myrna Nelson the night before. "I'm too nosy. I'm not a detective. I should have listened to you months ago."

Jeremy ignored me. "Probably a suicide. That's what Marv thinks. So does Myrna Nelson. Guess we're just waiting on the autopsy from the ME, but I lean towards them being right."

I stared at Jeremy for a few moments, trying to decipher the pleased looked on his face.

"Why are you still talking about it?" I asked.

"Why not?" Jeremy shrugged. "It's nothing you don't already know. Myrna Nelson sure was touched by the sympathy casserole you dropped by last night."

Rolling my eyes—not out of spite, but out of the exasperation of being caught—I groaned.

"Look, Germ, I—"

"You just couldn't. Could you?" Jeremy snorted out a laugh and shook his head. "You *had* to go over there and insert yourself in—"

"Okay!" I stammered. "I get it. I've felt like the worst person in the world since I went over there, all right? As soon as she started talking about Carter and...I realized I was torturing the woman because I just had to be up in everyone's business. I just had to know what was going on in the investigation. I get it now. All right? I barely slept last night because of how much I hated myself. Give me a break, Germ."

Trying not to grin, Jeremy finally nodded.

"So," he said, "lesson learned? You'll stop all this nonsense from here on out?"

"Yes!" I howled pitifully and sat back in my booth, thoroughly chastised.

After a few breaths passed and Jeremy was satisfied that I was beaten down far enough that the lesson had sunk in, he sighed.

"You didn't tell Myrna I'd brought the casserole under false pretenses," I asked, "did you?"

Jeremy found that incredibly amusing.

"You mean did I tell her that you aren't really a sympathetic, lovely young man who felt bad for her and only brought her a casserole because you happened to have one and it was a way to butt in on her business?"

"Uh…yeah."

"No," Jeremy said. "I let her believe you're a nice person."

I chuckled nervously.

"Sorry about ditching you last night," Jeremy said casually. "Work stuff."

I gave an upward nod.

"How is *work stuff*?" I asked.

He frowned at me. "Don't do that."

"Do what?"

"Point out my vagueness by being vague."

"I vaguely remember you telling me that I'm not a detective and to keep my nose out of other people's business," I said, amused. "So…I'm letting you play mysterious detective. I should get some credit for that."

The tip of Jeremy's shoe lightly tapped my shin under the table. We both chuckled. When he lowered his foot, the toe of his shoe rested on mine for a moment, and our eyes connected, then the sound of the sole scuffing against the linoleum as he pulled it away broke our concentration. I cleared my throat and rolled my neck, as though working out a crick.

"So," I said, my voice a little hoarser than I would have liked, "how are things down at the P.D.? Getting all the bad guys?"

"We do our best," Jeremy said.

"Good."

Fortunately, Shirley showed up at our tableside to take our orders, distracting us from the sudden, and odd, uneasiness. Well, she took Jeremy's order. She quoted mine to me and didn't even ask if it was right before walking away. I would have been offended except she had gotten it right. Like always.

For a few moments, Jeremy and I sat there, not exactly not looking at each other, but obviously trying not to stare at each other. I'm not an idiot. Jeremy and I had known each other since we were kids. Born and raised in Head Rock Harbor together. The only time we had spent apart was when I'd gone off to college for four years and he'd stayed home to sign up for the academy. However, once I'd come home and taken over the bookstore from my newly deceased aunt who had willed it to me, we were thick as thieves again.

Over all of those years, save the four, there had been...*something*...between us. A casual flirtation or two. Playfulness that didn't quite fit with a mere friendship. But we'd never acted on it. Jeremy liked to play the field and I was a romantic. We weren't a fit. So, we were friends. We'd never so much as held hands or given each other a brief, awkward kiss when we were teens.

We. Were. Just. Friends.

My throat was dry.

When Shirley arrived with my soda and Jeremy's sweet tea, I guzzled half mine without thinking. Finally, when she stepped away for the second time, I realized that what was happening was ridiculous. This was Jeremy. Even if we were in one of our more ridiculous awkward flirtatious periods with each other, we didn't have to act like we didn't know how to have a conversation.

Things were weird enough, seeing that the murder I'd solved in early Spring included the revelation that his boyfriend at the time was the murderer. The fact that Jeremy barely kept his boyfriend from stabbing me to death added to the awkwardness of the situation. Of course, that would make things weird between us for a while. Jeremy felt guilty. He was also now single. Stuff like that can throw a wrench in the works for a while.

"So," I said, "you were kind of weird yesterday."

Jeremy's brow furrowed.

"*Stay away from Sawyer,*" I did my best imitation of him. "What's that about?"

I reached for my soda and realized that I was possibly bringing up something that would make things exponentially more awkward. Jeremy looked down at his folded hands on the table.

"That was dumb," he said. "Sawyer's a…he's a stand-up guy. There's no reason you need to stay clear of him."

"It was weird." I repeated.

Jeremy shrugged. "Sorry, Jacks. I…yeah. I don't know."

"All right," I said, looking away for a moment. "So, now that Sawyer and I are obviously not the killers, I expect an apology for having to strip down to my skivvies in front of Deacon Davis in the middle of the bookstore."

Jeremy's eyes grew wide and he barely suppressed a laugh.

"You...*what?*" He gasped.

"He did the test on my hands then made me hand over my clothes, Germ," I said, unamused. "To have them tested for gun powder or some nonsense."

"Wait, wait, wait," Jeremy said, still suppressing a laugh. "Didn't I tell you to have your clothes ready for him? Then you wouldn't have to strip down?"

"No," I said, "you didn't."

Jeremy pushed his laughter away completely, but his cheeks grew red with effort.

"Sorry, Jacks."

"I'm sure you are."

"Just consider it payback for all of your sass and buttinsky behavior over the years," he said.

"Noted," I said. "I'll start planning your comeuppance for all of your annoying habits over the years."

Jeremy kicked my shin again, but he didn't let his foot fall onto mine. We both smiled, wordlessly forgiving each other. Shirley arrived with our platters and we dug into our meals. As we ate, we fell into the casual, easy conversation that had been typical of our friendship over the years. It was easy to simply sit with Jeremy, eat, talk, and not feel awkward in those types of moments. By the end of the meal, we were both laughing and chatting as we always had before the unintended awkwardness.

Shirley caught Jeremy waving her over and visited with us for a few moments before accepting payment and a tip at the table. After she told us to have a good rest of the day, Jeremy began to shrug his jacket back on. Patiently, I waited for him to get ready to leave. Before we had a chance to slide out of the booth, Jeremy's phone dinged in his pocket, and fumbling impatiently, he pulled the device out.

I started to slide from the booth, preparing my exit, as Jeremy silently read the screen of his phone. When he muttered a curse under his breath, my eyes shot up to see him, red faced and flustered.

"What is it?" I asked.

"Nothing," he grumbled, shoving his phone back into his pocket.

"Germ?"

He sighed and reached up to forcefully brush his fingers through his curls.

"They've got Mavis down at the station," he sighed. "They're going to book her."

I gasped. "For Carter? That's ridiculous. You know—"

"Her GSR came back positive," Jeremy said.

"Well, yeah," I stammered. "She doesn't go long without shooing her shotgun at something. We both know that. She was never going to pass a—"

"*And*," Jeremy said, stopping me as he leveled me with a look, "they caught her down at Lukey's Pawn."

I frowned at him.

"So?"

"She was trying to sell a watch," Jeremy said blandly. "That belonged to Carter."

My previously devoured pork tenderloin started tap dancing at the back of my throat.

"They're going to charge her with murder, Jacks," Jeremy said.

"Germ…"

"I gotta go," Jeremy said, and began to slide from his booth.

Stuttering and stammering, I slid out of the booth and dashed around him to stop him from leaving Munchies.

"Let me go with you." I begged. "We both know she didn't do this."

"Jacks—"

"Please," I stared into Jeremy's eyes.

My best friend had a battle with the side of his brain that was employed by Head Rock Harbor as a detective. Taking me with him to the station when he'd been summoned about a murder suspect's arrest could land him in hot water with Marv. Simply telling me Mavis had been arrested before it was public knowledge was a faux pas. I could practically see him working out a scenario where taking me to the station would turn out well for him.

I hated that I'd asked it of him, but Mavis couldn't defend herself—credibly—against the accusations Marv was going to sling at her. She wouldn't even know to keep her mouth shut until she had a court-appointed attorney. She'd flap her gums until she was all hooked up to a battery the size of a pickup truck. She needed someone on her side immediately. Jeremy knew if he delivered that person to the station, it could mean his neck.

"Fine," Jeremy said. "Let's go."

Chapter Eight

The look on Marv's face when I burst into the station ten steps ahead of Jeremy could have melted concrete. Though I felt bad for Jeremy's inevitable butt chewing—especially since I was the cause—Marv had no power over me. He could neither fire me nor arrest me. I didn't work for him and I'd done nothing illegal. Yet. So, marching into the station and having him glare at me didn't slow me down one bit.

Before I said anything, I twisted and turned my head, looking for a sign of the woman that Head Rock Harbor's finest was trying to frivolously charge with murder. Of course, I should have known without looking that Mavis was not in the room. It was too quiet. Mavis would have been spitting and hollering and causing a scene. The lobby of the station was peaceful, if not a bit tense, at the moment.

Officer Ashley Riley was stationed at the corner desk—which was typical—turned in his office chair so he was facing the door. Marv was at the desk in the center of the room, leaned back, half-sitting on its top, glaring at me. I could hear Gloria down the hallway, but her voice sounded muffled. She was probably starting the prayer chain now that a suspect had been arrested in the death of Carter Nelson.

I never understood why Marv could get so prickly with me being a bit nosy about police business in our little river town. Like everyone else in town I could get a little too interested in things that weren't my business. However, his employees were the main source of most of the gossip. If he wanted to keep things under a tight lid, he should have been more worried about Gloria, and stopped getting grumpy with bored citizens of Head Rock Harbor.

"Where's Mavis?" I asked, coming to stand in the center of the lobby as Jeremy ducked into the station behind me.

Marv glared at me for a moment, then shot a look over my shoulder when Jeremy appeared.

"You bring him here?" Marv barked.

"I saw his text while he was in the bathroom at Munchies," I replied. "We were having lunch. Don't go blaming him for my nosiness."

Going through Jeremy's phone while he was in the bathroom was something even I wasn't nosy enough to do. However, Marv believed I was a busybody of the highest order, so I was going to let him keep on believing it. Especially if it could keep Jeremy out of hot water.

I'm not certain what Jeremy did, but from the look on Marv's face as he stared over my shoulder at his detective told me he believed my story. He no longer looked angry at Jeremy, simply annoyed with me. If that's the worst that would come from Jeremy bringing me to the station with him, I was more than happy to deal with it.

"Why are you here?" Marv barked again.

"My daddy saw my momma across the smoky haze of a roadside biker bar and they both lost their sense for the night," I snipped. "They still haven't found it."

The corner of Marv's mouth turned up for the briefest of moments, then he was scowling once again. Jeremy rounded me, patting my shoulder as he went by. I waited patiently as he joined Marv at the center desk.

"Nosy over here saw the text," Jeremy said apologetically. "At that point there was no reason in not letting him come. He'd have shown up anyway. You know you can't keep Jackson from thinking he's a detective."

It stung, hearing those words come out of Jeremy's mouth. Even though I knew there was a little truth to them— at least as far as everyone else in the room was concerned— I also knew that he had said them to keep the ruse going. There'd be a time and place where I could chew Jeremy out for his choice of words, but while I was trying to get to see Mavis was not that time or place.

"Shut it," I said to Jeremy, jabbing a finger at him. "Where's Mavis, Marv?"

"She's in a cell," Marv waggled his head at me. "Old bird can't act right, so she's gonna sit there and calm down. She'll sit there *until* she calms down. Come summer and the sun don't shine, she's going to learn to act right!"

"You'd get water home from the well with a fish basket quicker, Marv," I said.

Again, he strained to not smile. Jeremy and Riley were not so discreet.

"She may be mean as all get out, Jackson," Marv growled, "but she's going to learn. One way or the other."

"You know she didn't do anything wrong."

"She was trying to sell a dead man's watch," Marv barked. "But you already know that, *detective*. Selling things that don't belong to you is *definitely wrong*."

"Did you even ask her where she got it?" I asked.

"Of course, I did!" Marv stammered. "But she told me where I could put it instead."

I wasn't as disciplined as Marv. Neither were Jeremy and Riley. We all grinned.

"I bet she did," I said, simply.

Marv waved me off angrily.

"She's in that cell. She's going to be in that cell. And she'll stay in that cell," Marv said, a touch of the anger gone from his voice. "Even if she doesn't talk, *bare minimum*, she's getting booked for theft!"

"Fine," I said. "Book her. What's her bail?"

Jeremy shrank, moving to sit atop the desk, giving a clear line from Marv to me. I didn't blame him. If I wanted to keep my job, I'd have done the same thing.

"You can't bail her out!" Marv's face was suddenly like a beet. "There's still the matter of the man's death, and—"

"And you have nothing to prove she had anything to do with it," I said. "Round up ten random people in this town and see if they pass a GSR test right now. Do it, Marv. At least fifty percent will fail."

Marv was sputtering, his head looking as though it might pop like a kernel of corn.

"She's not required to tell you anything. *She has the right to remain silent* and—"

"Which she's been anything but!" Marv growled.

"And you have nothing to book her for murder. So…book her for theft. I'll wait. What's the bail?"

"Don't you have a bookstore to run?" Marv demanded. "Don't you have anything to do beside be a splinter under my nail? Get out of here and go mind your business, Jackson. You ain't leavin' here with Mavis Attberry, and that's final!"

I didn't bother reminding Marv that Head Rock Harbor Books was closed half a day on Tuesdays and Wednesdays.

"That's unconstitutional," I said.

"Actually," Jeremy said, meekly, "a judge sets the bail, Jacks. Marv can book her for theft and keep her until a judge can arraign her. Tomorrow at the earliest since it's past lunch today."

I glowered at him. I *had* known that. However, I was hoping I'd have flustered Marv enough to get him to let me bail Mavis out of the jail. She wasn't going to survive a day or two behind bars. She wouldn't be the same person—for better or worse—after. However, Jeremy's defense of him put a smug grin on Marv's face, and I was glad that it would probably save Jeremy from Marv's wrath once I left.

"Fine," I bit the word off. "I'll sit here until tomorrow morning. I'll go to the arraignment. I'll bail her out right after."

All three officers rolled their heads back to stare at the ceiling.

"You are a blister on my butt," Marv groaned.

"Tell you what, Marv," I said. "Let me go back there and see her. Make sure she's okay and understands what's going on. Then I'll leave. *Until* I come to bail her out."

Though I knew Marv's head was going to nearly explode, I also knew that he would do anything to get me out of the station. Even if he had to concede and let me visit Mavis for a few minutes, he wanted me out more than he wanted to fight. I'd known Marv since I was a kid and he was a new recruit to the Head Rock Harbor Police Department. My parents had caused enough trouble during my upbringing that it would have been impossible for us to not be familiar with each other by the time I was grown.

He could be a hot head at times, but he wasn't so arrogant that he couldn't see reason.

"Five minutes, Jackson," Marv said finally, jabbing a finger at me. "Then you get out of here. I don't want to see you at this station until she has seen a judge."

"Fine," I said.

I said the word coolly, but internally I was relieved.

"Take him back there, Riley," Marv barked. "Let him see the old bird. *For five minutes.*"

Officer Ashley Riley rose from his seat at the corner desk and ran his hands over the front of his uniform slacks.

"All right, Chief," he replied.

Riley looked over at me and cocked his head towards the metal door that led from the lobby into the holding cell area. Without another word or look at Marv, I nodded at Riley and followed him to the far side of the lobby to the door. Jeremy and I glanced at each other, but avoided saying anything or even acknowledging each other with a change in our facial expressions. Even though I'd done my best to deflect blame from Jeremy, Marv was going to be contentious for a while. I didn't want to make things worse.

Officer Riley opened the holding cell door and slid it open, waving an arm to gesture me inside. I stepped through the doorway and Riley followed me. He didn't bother shutting the door behind us. Head Rock Harbor isn't that big of a town. Less than five thousand people reside within what is considered its city limits. Obviously, due to that fact, there aren't many holding cells in the Head Rock Harbor Police Department.

If, for some reason, prisoners needed to be held for a considerable length of time, or there are more people under arrest than the six cells in the station could handle, Marv took prisoners to the Jackson County Jail. That was a fairly uncommon occurrence, fortunately. Even with two murders in as many months, Head Rock Harbor was a safe and quiet community. Other than the occasional drunk and disorderly or fist fight down at Bernie's Tavern, there wasn't much to arrest folks for in our little town.

Mavis was in the third cell on the right. Each side of the long hallway had three cells, and they'd given her the furthest one from the lobby. Without asking, I'd known why. If she got riled up, her screams and hollers would less likely be audible that far away and with the metal door between the cells and the lobby. Fortunately, Mavis was the only prisoner currently housed in the station. No one else was going to suffer her wrath for the time being.

"There she is," Officer Riley gestured vaguely at the cell. "Five minutes."

"All right," I said.

He walked back down the short hallway to the lobby, leaving the metal door at the end wide open. Standing in front of the cell, looking through the bars, my eyes finally landed on Mavis. To the left side of the cell was a toilet and sink hung on the wall. On the right side was a metal bed, anchored to the wall, a flimsy, thin, sheet-covered pad barely thick enough to qualify as a mattress lay upon. An anorexic pillow covered in a threadbare case was at the end of the bed closest to the bars.

Mavis was seated on the bed, her feet on the cell floor. She had turned so that she wasn't quite looking away from the bars, but I couldn't see her face. It had surprised me when she hadn't cursed out Officer Riley when we approached, but she had never really had a problem with Ashley. No one did. He followed Marv's orders too quickly, but there was no ill will between him and members of the community. He did his job and paid his bills. You couldn't fault a person for that.

"Mavis?" I said softly. "It's Jackson."

Mavis, a slightly dumpy woman, short in stature with the posture of a bridge troll jerked slightly at the sound of my voice. Her wine-colored hair—straight from monthly visits from Miss Clairol—needed a good brush. She'd been arrested, fortunately, in one of her standard plaid button-down short-sleeve shirts, dungarees, and foam rubber clogs. When she turned slowly to look at me, I immediately saw that the right lens in her browline glasses had been cracked. If it hadn't been for the look of fire and brimstone on her face, I'd have felt horrible for her.

"You okay, Mavis?" I asked.

"They took all my jewelry!" Mavis exclaimed. "My bracelet! My necklace!"

Mavis's "jewelry" was a cheap thin gold chain she wore around her neck along with a matching bracelet. I didn't think that Marv was going to Lukey's with her belongings.

"They do that," I said. "When you get arrested. They'll give them back to you when you bail out. I'll make sure of it."

"*They was my memaw's!*" Mavis threw her head back and bellowed. "*Marv Bucksworth! I curse your whole bloodline! I curse your daughter for being unfortunate enough to be born to ya'! I—*"

Marv stomped to the doorway at the other end of the hall and cut her off with his own screams.

"*Visiting time will be over right this instant and I'll make sure you rot in that cell, Mavis, if you don't shut up!*"

Mavis's face twisted into a glower as she stared in the direction of the door, though she couldn't see it from where she was seated. But she said nothing else. After a moment, Marv spoke again.

"*Good!*" Then he stomped away from the door again.

I shook my head as the sound of Marv's footsteps drew further away. Mavis was still glowering, so I gave her a moment to collect herself. With only five minutes to talk to her, I didn't want to waste time, but I knew enough about Mavis to know she wasn't coherent when really angry.

She was always angry. *Really* angry was another creature.

"Mavis," I said when her glower went away and was replaced with a frown, "what happened? Where—"

"I didn't kill that man!" she announced. "I didn't even know about that dead man until they came and brought me in for that godforsaken hand swipin' test!"

"Okay," I said. "Okay. I know you didn't."

"And someone's going to have to check on my tomatoes!" Mavis barked. "If I ain't there to care for 'em—"

Mavis didn't grow tomatoes. But she did have plants that grew alongside tomatoes brilliantly. Everyone knew about Mavis's plants. I suspected even Marv knew. We all kept our mouths shut and looked the other way. Her *drinking* was the problem. As long as Mavis only grew enough plants for personal use, it wasn't worth addressing.

"You'll be out of here tomorrow," I said, shushing her. "Your plants will be fine until then."

Mavis's face squinched up and her eyes turned to slits, but she seemed to accept that what I said was the truth. I'd never lied to her before, after all.

"Mavis," I asked, "where did you find Carter Nelson's watch?"

"Who?" she snapped.

"The dead man?"

"I done told that old fool out there," she waved towards the station lobby, "that I found it on the trail behind the park. Finders keepers! I didn't steal nothin'."

My brow furrowed as I thought of the hiking trail that went through part of Wilford Woods, around Harper's Trailer Park, and around Harper's Bar, Grill, Bait & Tackle to the main road. It was a leisurely walk along the trail, spanning less than three miles. A lot of folks hiked the trail on the weekends, or took it through the woods out to fish or camp.

When tourists came to town and ate at Harper's at lunch, many of them would often take the hike after their meal. Even townies used it to get in some exercise from time to time. It made sense that if Carter and his son...*Colton?*...had been camping out in Wilford Woods, they might have taken the trail from time to time.

"When'd you find it?" I asked.

"Just this morning," Mavis replied with a harrumph. "Real nice, too. Took it straight to Lukey's because he don't ask no questions."

Apparently, Lukey had broken that rule. There was no other way Marv would have found out that Mavis was at the pawn shop with property that didn't belong to her. I'd have to have a word with Lukey when I had time.

"Is that all?" I asked.

"I ain't seen nothin' else," Mavis insisted. "And I ain't killed nobody, either!"

"I know you didn't, Mavis," I said, reassuringly. "Listen, they only gave me five minutes to talk to you and that was pushing it."

I stepped up to the bars and held onto them as I whisper-hissed to her, hoping that Marv wouldn't hear us. Making him angrier with what I was about to advise Mavis to do was not going to help the situation.

"Look," I said, "they'll take you in front of the judge tomorrow to set your bail. They don't have anything to charge you with murder. Just, possibly, theft. Marv's on a trip."

"You ain't tellin' me nothin' new."

I cracked a smile. "You let the judge set your bail, and I'll get you out. Mind your manners and don't back talk to the judge. Okay?"

"I'll do my best," she snarled.

"I'm serious, Mavis," I said. "You be your best self to that judge or you'll be in this cell 'til God knows when and your plants will die. And you'll have to start from seed all over. Okay?"

That straightened Mavis's face. I'd known her long enough to know how to get her to pay attention. After a moment of consideration, she nodded firmly once.

"Then I'll bail you out and we'll get this all straightened out," I said. "Okay?"

"Yeah. All right. But you can't be spending all your hard-earned money—"

"You let me worry about my money, okay?" I cut her off. "And for the love of everything, don't answer any questions from Marv, Jeremy, Ashley—none of them. Okay? They send a lawyer or someone in here, you keep your mouth shut. Understood? You only talk to the judge and when you do, you use your manners. And if you can manage it, don't irritate Marv while you're here."

Mavis didn't look happy about it, but she finally gave me another curt nod.

"All right," I said. "I'm going to go and see if there's anything I can do for you. I'll see you tomorrow. I promise."

Mavis didn't say anything, but she nodded again, then turned back to how'd she'd been sitting before I arrived. Knowing there was nothing else I could say that would soothe her, I dropped my hands from the bars, gave her one last look, and turned away. I marched down the hallway, through the doorway, and back into the lobby.

Officer Riley was waiting to slide the metal door into place. He latched it with a loud "clang" as I stood there, frowning at Marv as he continued to perch on the desk in the middle of the room. Jeremy hopped from the desk and came over to me, grabbing me around the shoulders. As he led me from the door leading into the holding cells to the front door of the station, my head turned to keep my gaze on Marv. He didn't blink. Neither did I.

Finally, when Jeremy pushed the lobby door open to the outside, he gave me a nudge and pushed me out of the station. My eyes finally went to him as the brisk breeze ruffled my hair. Though the look on his face was one of sympathy, I wasn't sure if it was for me, Mavis, or himself. I had definitely put him in a spot.

"*Please go home,*" Jeremy pleaded with me quietly.

He gave me one last look, then closed the door.

And I was standing there, wondering how Marv could call *this* justice.

Chapter Nine

Wednesday began similarly to Tuesday in that I had been unable to sleep well all night long. Thinking about Mavis stuck in her spartan jail cell all night long, erroneously suspected of murder, and wondering if Marv would ever get some sense had me tossing and turning all night long. Knowing that I'd put Jeremy in a tough spot at work had added to the anxiety pile. However, it was either put Jeremy in a tight spot or let Mavis get railroaded by the Head Rock Harbor justice system. Such as it was.

There had only been one right choice.

Standing up for Mavis when no one else would had not only been kind, it had been right.

The most surprising thing upon waking Wednesday morning had been the short, direct text from Jeremy.

Don't bother coming up here today. Mavis was let out. The Nelson family didn't want to press charges.

No explanation was given in the text as to why the Nelson family wouldn't want to press charges against a woman accused of stealing their dead relative's watch. The idea that a family wouldn't press charges in such a situation had a frown plastered to my face as I went about my morning routine. Rattlesnatches' bowl got filled. I showered. I made breakfast. The furrow in my brow only got deeper and deeper.

I'm not an unforgiving person. In fact, as far as transgressions go, I've forgiven plenty in my day. However, I couldn't see not pressing charges against a person who tried to pawn my dead father's watch. Especially if they were a possible suspect and my father had been found dead within the last day. I wasn't a Nelson, though. I was a Harper. We hold grudges better than most if we really put our minds to it.

By the time I'd opened the store for the day, I'd done my best to push those thoughts out of my head. Mavis was out of jail. I wouldn't have to post bail money for her. As far as I knew, she wasn't being charged with murder. Everything had turned out okay. There was no point in ruining the whole day scowling about something that had resolved itself. Even if there was a little voice in the back of my head telling me something wasn't right.

The Nelsons didn't want to press charges?

That was odd.

But everything was back to square one. Mavis was out of jail and back at home. She wasn't facing any charges anymore—for the time being. The Nelson family, obviously, felt that Carter had committed suicide and there was no reason to suspect anyone else of wrong doing. Even after all of the GSR tests, the attempt to pawn Carter's watch, and the odd feeling in my gut, we simply had a dead man in the woods with a likely self-inflicted gunshot wound.

My gut still didn't feel right, though.

Fortunately—depending upon how you looked at things—I didn't have much of my morning to decipher what was tickling my gray matter. Shortly after ten, when the bookstore was devoid of customers for once during the morning, the bell clanged loudly. Linda Wagner, her arms cradling a binder to her chest, entered the store. Her husband, Mark, anxiously trailed in behind her. Having the mayor of Head Rock Harbor, and her husband, show up at the bookstore never brightened my day.

"Good morning, Linda," I said, looking up from my laptop briefly to greet her. "Are you looking for a specific book?"

I knew Linda wasn't looking for a book. Neither was Mark. The town mayor and her husband had never once purchased a book from my store. However, one could always hope that distracting the mayor would get her to leave quicker.

"Jackson," Linda said as she walked up to the counter and laid the binder down, "I've brought over the plans for the Pride celebration for June."

Glancing down at the navy-blue binder, I saw the small rainbow sticker affixed to its cover.

"Well," I said, leveling her with my eyes, "it's good to have everything planned out."

Linda Wagner had been hounding me for at least two years to help plan an annual Pride parade for Head Rock Harbor. Ever since I'd returned to college, she had labeled me the town mascot when it came to all things LGBTQIA. Naturally, as the town mascot, having me in charge of the inaugural Pride parade made sense in her mind.

"I hope it all goes well for you," I added.

Our mayor stared blankly at me, unamused. After a moment, she pushed the binder a few inches closer to me on the counter.

"Use what I, along with the City Council, have framed out in here to plan the parade," Linda said. "We've outlined a budget."

I gave the binder another glance.

"Pass."

"*Jackson Harper, I—*"

"Linda Wagner," I interjected, "I've told you time and time again that I am not interested in planning the Pride parade. There are other members of the LGBTQIA community in this town who would be more than happy to help you."

I nudged the binder to the edge of the counter on her side.

"I have a business to run," I said. "I don't have time—"

"None of those community members owns a business on Harbor Street," Linda interrupted me. "None of them have the relationship you have with other business owners on this street. You are in the perfect position to convince other business owners on the street to decorate for the parade, participate fully, and support a new local tradition."

"Pass."

It's not that I didn't care about the Pride parade and festivities Mayor Wagner had in mind. In fact, I cared very much how Head Rock Harbor implemented a new local tradition of celebrating Pride every year. As a gay man, I fully agreed that implementing a Pride month celebration into the city's yearly events was overdue and needed. Seeing my hometown and its citizens parade through town and declare that love was love meant a lot to me. However, being labeled "Head Homosexual" by our mayor felt icky.

Linda's severe, yet colorful pantsuit, her bob haircut that meant business, and Mark's lime green Polo, matched with his khaki slacks, made me wonder if they weren't already dressed for Pride. They were more colorful than I, in my forest green sweater and black jeans. Of course, I had to wonder if they had dressed the way they had to further try to convince me to get involved with the parade planning.

"Get Jeremy," I said. "He can get the police involved and—"

"Your mother has shown interest in taking charge," Linda said, a poisonous smile creeping up her face.

"*What?*" I squinted at her.

"Deborah said she would *love* to help plan the Pride activities." The words oozed from Linda's lacquered lips. "She said she had plenty of ideas to—"

I snatched the binder from the counter and held it to my chest.

"That's low, Linda," I glowered at her. "Even for a politician."

She smiled at me as I tried to use my mind powers to melt the face from her skull. Mark seemed to shrink behind his wife, drawing himself out of the line of fire.

Linda had known exactly what she was doing by asking my mother to participate in the planning of a Pride event. My mother, full of faults as she was, had more pride in her son than one mother had the right. If she was in charge of planning the first Pride event, it would be the most over the top, cartoonish, and unintentionally offensive parade of all time. And somehow, I'd still be the town mascot for the LGBTQIA community.

"I didn't become mayor by being subtle," Linda sniffed.

I frowned. "After I plan this parade, my next order of business is to support your opponent in the next election."

Linda cackled.

"See you in three years!" She exclaimed as she turned on her heels, nearly knocking Mark over.

I continued to stare daggers at Linda as she marched to the front door, Mark scuttling behind her. When they had exited the shop and the door was closed, the clanging of the bell still echoing through the shop, I dropped the binder on the counter. Grumbling and annoyed, I stared down at the cutesy rainbow sticker affixed to the front. There was still time to chase Linda down, declare that I would *never* be interested in planning the parade, and shove the binder back into her nasty little arms.

And she'd go right to Deb. Linda Wagner had no desire to let Deb plan any major event in town that would attract tourists. She knew as well as I did that it would garner the wrong kind of attention. However, she'd take the loss simply to spite me.

A parade around the square, down Harbor Street, ending at the harbor.

A little picnic for everyone. Maybe Lardell and Beau will cook barbecue?

Live music? Fireworks in the evening?

Maybe a parade of boats on the river by the harbor?

All the business owners on Harbor Street would probably at least hang rainbow flags and streamers...

I snatched the binder off of the counter and stuffed it underneath. Thinking about the Pride parade in two months was not what I had planned for my day. In another fit, I ripped the binder out from under the shelf and tucked it under my arm. With a harrumph that would make Mel Brooks proud, I headed to the front door. Rattlesnatches lifted his head from his napping spot on the check-out counter long enough to decide he did not approve of my antics, then went right back to sleep.

End of day—and my lunch period—was a few minutes off still, but I decided that, as owner of Head Rock Harbor Books, I could do whatever I liked. Slapping the lights off on my way out, I exited the shop, locking the door behind me. Marching like a man on a mission, I made my way down Harbor Street to Munchies. Nothing could clear my head and ease my pain as I went over the binder of material for the Pride ideas Linda had like Lardell's cooking.

As I entered Munchies, I found the diner empty, considering the early hour. I nodded at Shirley, and it was understood that she'd put in my regular order. She smiled and gestured for me to take a seat, so I helped myself to the booth in the back corner. I could hear Lardell, the owner of Munchies—and Shirley's father—start up my order in the kitchen as I flipped the binder open on the table.

When my pork tenderloin, fries, coleslaw, and a side of ranch came out, I'd had enough time to go through half the binder. Linda's ideas for Pride looked as if she expected a gaggle of gay men to eat Skittles and then regurgitate the half-digested candies all over town. I don't particularly have anything against color or rainbows, but there was a level of taste that was lacking with Linda's ideas. Of course, if you leave Pride planning to anyone but the gays, you end up with a commercial, capitalist mess full of unicorns and rainbows and no real substance.

Eating with one hand, I used a pen I borrowed from Shirley to cross out tons of Linda's ideas. Jotting in notes here and there, I did what I could with what Linda had provided, hoping I could salvage at least a few of her ideas. If I didn't do anything Linda wanted, it would be worse than refusing to plan the event completely.

When I looked up from my empty plate an hour later, I'd worked my way through the entire binder—which was full of scratched out lines and jotted notes. Munchies had also filled up without me even noticing. Every table in the joint was full and the room was filled with the boisterous laughter and conversations of locals. I shook my head, wondering how I had become so engrossed in the Pride plans that I hadn't noticed the noise and crowd.

With a sigh, I closed the binder and patted my belly, realizing I hadn't needed to eat *every single thing* on my plate. However, Lardell's cooking was simply too good to not devour every morsel of his Midwestern delicacies. As I slid from the booth, the binder tucked under my arm once more, I noticed the booth by the front window was occupied by four men.

The Nelson boys.

I paused, watching the four men eating quietly at the window, wondering what had brought them to Munchies. Usually, in times such as the death of a loved one, so much food is brought to a family that eating out is unnecessary. Additionally, I realized that the fourth man in the booth was Colton, Carter's son. He was easy to pick out of the line up since I already knew the other Nelsons. Forlorn, his shoulders slumped as he picked at the food on his plate, I couldn't help but feel bad for the guy. They were all dressed in Carhartt, as though ready to go out to the deer stand the minute they finished their meals.

Colton Nelson didn't look much younger than me. I wasn't sure if his mother was still alive, but losing either parent at such a young age didn't seem right. Parents are supposed to die before their children, obviously, but we all expect them to live until we're at least seventy or eighty years old, right? Resolutely, I rose from the booth and made my way over to the front of the diner. Several people gave me a nod or a greeting of some kind as I passed their tables, and I returned their gestures in kind.

After paying Shirley at the check-out counter and having a quick chat about the going's on in town, I turned my attention to the window booth. The four Nelson boys were still picking at their lunch, the only table in the place that was dead silent. Before I could talk myself out of it, I made my way over to their table.

"Hey, guys," I said as a greeting.

All of the Nelson boys, except Colton, looked up at me. Kenny, the eldest of the brood, spoke up for the group.

"Oh," he said, "hey, Jackson."

I nodded. "I just wanted to say how sorry I was about Carter. I know there's never a good time—especially when you're trying to enjoy a meal—but I wanted to pay my condolences."

Colton glanced at me, then back at his food.

"That's kind of you, Jackson," Kenny said. "Ma said you're the one that brought that casserole over the other night."

"It was really good," Mason added. "Thank you."

It hurt my heart seeing hellraisers like the Nelson boys so glum. Kenny and I were the same age and had been in practically every class together in high school. His brothers were barely trailing behind us, so I knew them from the hallways of the school as well. Seeing them so out of sorts—and out of character—I was unnerved. They'd always been class clowns, hellraisers, or whatever label you wanted to apply that was similar.

"You're welcome," I said.

"It's…been tough," Kenny said, reaching up to scratch at his chin whiskers as he looked out the front window. "But we'll get through it. Family does that."

"Sure," I said, realizing I had already overstayed my welcome at their table. "Well, anyway, sorry again."

They all nodded. Except Colton. Before I had a chance to step away, one more thought entered my head.

"Oh," I said quietly, "and thank you for not pressing charges against Mavis. I really appreciate that. She may not say so, but I'm sure she appreciates it, too."

Colton twitched in his seat. Kenny, Mason, and Hunter exchanged glances.

"Well," Kenny said slowly, "we knew we couldn't send her to jail for something she didn't do."

I stared back at him. Sometimes, if you don't respond, people keep talking. Kenny was no exception to that train of thought.

"Carter was always losing things," he said as a way of explanation. "He probably just dropped his watch going up to Harper's. That's all."

"Y'all went to my mom's place?" I asked, smiling.

All of the boys seemed to fidget in their seats.

"Yeah," Hunter said, glancing at Kenny. "The night...well. The night Carter shot himself."

"Oh," I said.

I wanted to ask if the food was that bad, but felt it was in poor taste. Comedy equals tragedy plus time. There simply hadn't been enough time. Only tragedy. However, I've always felt that comedy was also accuracy without tact.

"I guess he didn't like her place," I said.

Fortunately, all of the boys, save Colton, chuckled.

"He didn't come," Mason said. "He was going to walk up with us from the campsite, but he got mad and—"

"He decided to go back to camp," Kenny finished his brother's thought. "He probably dropped his watch on the walk. Mavis picked it up. Not her fault."

"I see," I said.

Actually, I didn't see. However, whatever the boys thought in order to keep Mavis out of jail was all right by me.

"Well," I said, "my condolences once again. Let your mom know I can whip up another casserole if needed."

The Nelsons all took turns saying "thank you" and some form of "goodbye"—except for Colton—and I made my way out of Munchies, giving Shirley a final wave.

On my short walk back to the bookstore, my gut was clenching in tiny little knots. As it always did when there was something tickling my brain that I couldn't quite figure out. I was so engrossed in my thoughts that Linda's binder nearly slipped from its spot under my arm a half dozen times in the two blocks back to the store. I did my best to clear my head of the intrusive thoughts and tucked the binder more tightly under my arm.

By the time I reached the store, I was singing nursery rhymes in my head to ignore anything to do with Carter's death. I put the key in the lock and turned it, thinking about little lambs and cows that jumped over the moon. Surely, if something was fishy about Carter's death, the police would have found it. So far, the only thing they'd found was a bogus reason to throw Mavis Attberry in jail for less than one night. I simply had to let it go. There was nothing about Carter Nelson's death that had anything to do with me.

I didn't bother turning on the lights when I entered the bookstore. I simply shut the door behind me and relocked it since the store was closed for the rest of the day. I continued singing tunes in my head as I returned my keys to the hook by the door. So distracted by my attempts to ignore my own thoughts, I realized too late that I was not alone in the store. Before I could even take a breath, I realized someone was standing in the shadows at the check-out counter.

That's what you get for not paying attention.

Chapter Ten

Gasping and clutching my chest, I grumbled, *"What are you doing in here?"*

Jeremy, leaning against the counter, one elbow atop it, was being observed by Rattlesnatches, who was still curled up in a ball by the register. With the lights out in the shop, Jeremy's face was cast in shadow, leaving his expression a mystery. However, once my eyes began to adjust to the gloom, I realized he was staring blankly at me. For a moment, he stared at me, then he turned slightly to scratch Rattlesnatches' head with his other hand.

"You are incorrigible," he said simply.

"Pardon?"

"I saw you talking to the Nelsons at Munchies," he said. "Saw you through the window. You just can't leave well enough alone, can you?"

"I was paying my condolences!" I snapped. "What are you doing in here? How'd you get in here?"

"You gave me a key, Sherlock." Jeremy patted his hip pocket. "You want to play detective but you can't even figure out that mystery?"

"Well," I said, "now I want it back."

I held my hand out, my other hand going to my waist.

Jeremy scoffed. "No."

"No? *No?*"

"It's mine. You can't have it."

"Actually," I said, "it's *mine.*"

"Not anymore," Jeremy said, still scratching Rattlesnatches' head. "You gave it to me free and clear. And besides, if I don't have a key, how will I get in here the next time you get yourself in trouble and need rescuing?"

Sputtering, I tried to form words, but Jeremy ignored me, which made it impossible to think of something witty to say back.

"I wasn't bothering the Nelsons!" I finally managed.

"Okay," Jeremy said with a shrug. "Sure. You're still incorrigible."

"What are you doing in here?" I asked again. "Answer me."

"Well," Jeremy said, pushing away from the check-out counter, "if you must know, I saw you in Munchies through the window. And I needed to talk to you. But I felt that having a public conversation—that might get back to Marv—was a bad idea."

Gnawing at the corner of my lip, I suddenly felt bad. Jeremy had snuck into the bookstore so that no one would see us talking. Because I was on Marv's Naughty List.

"So, I came here to wait for you," Jeremy said. "I could tell you were on your way back here."

Feeling like the piece of garbage I possibly was, I slumped and went to stand at the counter, mirroring Jeremy's position by propping myself on one elbow against it. I kept space between us since I'd obviously put myself in a position where my physical nearness would not be welcome by my best friend. Deb's voice rang in my head, asking me why I couldn't mind my business. Why did I always have to be nosy? It was getting worse as time went along. By the time I was retired I'd be looking out the back window of my apartment with binoculars, calling the police about kids riding their bikes down the alley.

"Look, Germ," I began, "I'm sorry. It's just that—"

"Carter Nelson didn't commit suicide, Jacks," Jeremy stopped me. He didn't stop scratching Rattlesnatches' head and he didn't turn to look at me. "Anyone with half a brain could see that."

With wide eyes, I stared at my friend.

"But Marv...you know Marv," Jeremy said. "He's just...he's counting down the days until retirement. And— between you and me—Linda is not happy with him. Two murders in as many months? *In Head Rock Harbor?* She's worried about tourism, he's worried about retirement, and no one has time for complications. Carter Nelson is a complication. They both want to bury it with a neat little 'suicide bow'. *Throw a parade! Shut and closed case!*"

"What?" I whispered.

"What I want to know," Jeremy ignored my question, "is how you realized it wasn't suicide. Why you keep asking questions all the time. What made you realize there was something else going on?"

"What do you—"

"Because I know something isn't right, but I can't put the pieces together. And I'm the dang detective." Jeremy huffed a self-effacing laugh.

I thought about what Jeremy had said.

"What makes *you* think it's not suicide?" I asked. "I mean…it could be, right?"

Jeremy shrugged. "Just doesn't feel right. I mean…*a shotgun blast to the chest?* Not to be morbid, Jacks, but folks who choose a shotgun usually suck on the barrel. And it's hard to hold a shotgun to your chest and pull the trigger to begin with."

"Well—"

"Usually, people who choose that method sit down, propped up against something, and then suck on the barrel, and use their toe for the trigger. His boots were on. Carter was laying down when he was shot."

"How do you know?" I asked quietly, as if there was someone around to hear us.

"Forensics," Jeremy said, rolling his eyes goofily at me.

I couldn't help but laugh. Obviously, something in the forensics report had clued Jeremy in on angles and directions and blood splatter, and all that fun stuff that churned a person's guts.

"Okay," I said. "So, he was on the ground, laid out already when he took the blast to the chest. It's improbable but still possible that—"

"Jacks," Jeremy said, "don't stonewall me when you've been running around town playing detective. Don't be contrary."

"I'm not being contrary," I said. "You're being contrary. *You're a contrarian!*"

"You're always disagreeing with me for the sake of disagreeing." Jeremy's words were harsh but the smile on his face told me he wasn't trying to start a fight. "You enjoy disagreeing with me."

I shrugged. He was right. Arguing with Jeremy was a favorite pastime. I didn't know what that said about our friendship dynamic. It almost felt like...*foreplay*.

"It's fun," I said.

He smiled, his brilliant white teeth flashing in the gloom of the dark shop.

"So," he said, "how did you know it wasn't suicide?"

"I didn't." I admitted. "Something just didn't feel right. Then again, violent deaths aren't meant to feel right. Whether they're murder or suicide. My feelings could be making me think something that isn't really true."

"Fair," Jeremy said. "But forensics tell me that your gut might be onto something."

"Can you," I asked slowly, "get me a copy? Of the Medical Examiner's report?"

Jeremy looked at me like I was crazy.

"How am I supposed to help if I don't know what you know?" I asked.

He thought that over, his hand leaving Rattlesnatches' head. Through the shadows of the shop, he stared at me, unspeaking as he considered the ramifications of my request.

"Find something that makes me think I'm not crazy for thinking what I'm thinking," Jeremy said, "and I'll take the risk of bringing you a copy to read."

"Find what?" I chuckled. "Where would I even begin?"

Jeremy shrugged. "You figured it out with Prescott Pemberton. Figure this one out."

"Excuse me," I said, "but am I going to get a part of your salary for this, or what?"

Jeremy took his turn to chuckle.

"I'll take you out to The Dock for a steak dinner," Jeremy said, glancing away. "Anything you want. My treat."

"Wine included?" I asked quickly.

Jeremy nodded, his eyes returning to mine.

"Wine included."

A thought suddenly popped into my head.

"Why don't you tell Marv what you think?" I asked. "He's crotchety and getting more difficult as he counts down the days 'til he puts himself out to pasture, but he's not entirely unreasonable."

"Come on, Jacks," Jeremy shook his head, amused. "We both know that if he can write this whole thing off as a suicide and get it off the books, he's going to. Marv isn't a bad guy, but he's not going to pursue a case when the family is satisfied with the suicide narrative. He just doesn't have it in him anymore. He's tired and...he doesn't want Head Rock Harbor to be the murder capital of Iowa. If there's a surefire way to keep Linda Wagner on his butt, that would be it."

"I guess I can understand that."

"Marv," Jeremy sighed, taking a moment before continuing, "is driving me insane. He's why I've been so grumpy lately. It's impossible to get him to let us do real police work. He just wants to keep the status quo around here. *Don't write too many tickets. Don't pursue charges if it's not a severe crime. Don't do more work than necessary.* It's like he thinks Head Rock Harbor is a utopia that needs to be preserved."

"Then why'd he arrest Mavis the other night?" I stammered. "That was—"

"He's had it out for her for forever, Jacks," Jeremy said. "You know that. He has a soft spot for her, but she's been a thorn in his side for ages. He saw a chance to send her up the river for good. If he could get rid of his biggest troublemaker in town, he was going to risk a little bad publicity—like another murder. Now that Mavis is off the table—thanks to the Nelsons—suicide it is again."

I frowned, blowing a breath out through my nose violently.

"I know," Jeremy said. "I know."

"That's infuriating."

"Try working with him."

We both chuckled, and another thought occurred to me.

"You knew this the other day," I said slowly. "At the police station. When you told me to mind my business because you didn't want me to get hurt. You knew then that Carter didn't kill himself."

Jeremy gave a half shrug. "I wasn't certain. I hadn't read the report then. But I suspected something."

"So, what's changed? Now you want me to endanger myself?"

"No," Jeremy said. "I don't. But who am I going to ask for help? *Officer Ashley Riley*? He can't do his job without someone to hold his hand."

"Fair," I said. "So...a fine meal at The Dock *with wine* seems like a small reward for endangering myself. I think I might require a dessert with my meal as well."

Jeremy smiled. He reached out, paused, then continued with his movement and chucked me under the chin.

"You got it," he said.

Before I could ask anything else, Jeremy pushed away from the counter and rounded me to walk towards the front door. He stopped at my side and his hand went around my forearm. I stared down at his hand then up at him.

"Be careful, Jacks," he said softly. "Okay?"

I swallowed. "I always am."

Jeremy stared into my eyes for a moment, then his grip loosened on my arm and his hand slid away. As his hand slid down my arm, his fingertips played along the palm of my hand. I couldn't take my eyes off of his.

What was going on? For real?

Jeremy broke our eye contact finally and sauntered over to the front door. He unlocked it and reached for the knob. Before he opened the door, he looked over his shoulder at me.

"They've taken the police tape down out at the campsite," Jeremy said. "No one's watching it. Or the trail that leads up to Harper's. Just so you know."

"Got it," I said hoarsely.

Jeremy turned to the door, then looked over his shoulder again, as if a thought suddenly occurred to him.

"But, you know," he said, "try not to make a spectacle of yourself."

He gave me a wink and a smile, then he left. I watched as he closed and locked the door behind him. Maybe Jeremy having a key was useful after all.

The palm of my hand tingled where he ran his fingers.

Chapter Eleven

Rattlesnatches and I spent the rest of the afternoon and early evening in the bookstore and in our apartment upstairs. After Jeremy had left the bookstore, I found I was perplexed by more than a few things. First and foremost, I had to wonder how desperate Jeremy had to be to ask for my help in getting to the bottom of Carter Nelson's presumed suicide. Always insistent that he was the best detective in the Head Rock Harbor Police Department—even if there was only one—it was odd of him to want to share the spotlight.

That was Jeremy in his professional and personal life. I loved my friend dearly, but he did enjoy being the center of attention. Asking me to step into the spotlight with him was a rare request and left me wondering how bad things were at the police department. Had Marv gone completely 'round the bend in trying to sweep undesirable events in Head Rock Harbor under the rug? Or was Marv simply not going to advocate tilting at windmills?

It was entirely possible that Marv felt Carter Nelson's case was a simple case of suicide and further investigating was a waste of resources. There was nothing wrong with calling it like you see it, after all. Jeremy could also be right about everything feeling off about the suicide angle. Especially if the forensics report was as shady as he'd implied. Of course, I'd want to see the report for myself before I picked a side in that war.

Another thing that bothered me was my own attitude during the preceding days. It hadn't gone unnoticed by my brain that, well, my brain was sending negative signals every chance it got. I found myself wondering why I was aware of how grouchy I'd been, but at the same time, had been unable to put my attitude in check. Logically, I knew that I was experiencing trauma at having found the body of a man who had died under violent circumstances—suicide or not.

Yet another dead body.

I may not have been the person who found Prescott Pemberton's body out by the harbor when he had been murdered—but I'd found Marshelle Martin's—and the bodies seemed to be piling up. That and stress of seeing the trauma done to Carter Nelson's body by a shotgun blast had burrowed itself in my brain. As I thought about it, all I could picture was that hole in his chest, the blood, the unseeing, lifeless eyes staring up at the trees. His blotchy face. I cringed.

Obviously, I had been affected by the discovery of Carter Nelson's body at the campsite in the woods. Being a red-blooded man in America—gay or not—I'd "manned up" and pretended as though I was totally fine. However, I could no longer lie to myself. Finding a dead body in the woods is traumatic. Maybe I needed to deal with that before I could help Jeremy further? Before my attitude totally devolved into a grouchiness that was unbearable.

I nearly texted Sawyer to see how he felt since finding Carter Nelson, but decided against it. One thing I know about guys—unless you know them really well—it's not always welcome to ask them about their mental health. God forbid their feelings. Talking to Jeremy would be best. If I needed to talk to a friend. He'd understand. He wouldn't judge me or think I was weak.

Then again, did I have time to worry about dealing with my feelings before looking for clues? What if Jeremy was right and there was a killer loose in Head Rock Harbor? Not that my mental health wasn't important, but finding the killer would be more important in the short term.

Sitting at the kitchen table in my apartment, I took my time poring over my options. It occurred to me that I needed to strike a compromise with Jeremy. If he'd show me the forensics report to prove that there was something to be suspicious of, I would help him investigate. Delaying addressing my mental health required some proof that I was doing it for a good enough reason. Then again, asking Jeremy to jump the gun and risk his job to show me the forensics report could possibly affect my mental health further.

Knowing you're responsible for your friend losing their job doesn't feel good.

I imagine.

To distract myself during my afternoon glum-fest, I considered the hours of operation for Head Rock Harbor Books. Since I'd inherited the store from my aunt, right out of college, the hours had been the same. For nearly five years, Head Rock Harbor Books was typically open from nine in the morning until seven at night Mondays, Thursdays, Fridays, and Saturdays. From nine in the morning until noon on Tuesdays and Wednesdays, and closed on Sundays. It had been prickling at my mind that having two days off in a row each week would be nice.

With the money I made from the *Detective Randy Melton Mystery series*, I didn't even really need to run the bookstore. However, I loved the bookstore and enjoyed the day-to-day work. I loved the normalcy. *I loved books. I loved readers.* It also provided a cover for true profession as a reclusive and secretive best-selling author. Closing the bookstore was not an option. Having a "weekend" like other people was something I desperately wanted, though. Even if *my* weekend wasn't on the *actual* weekend.

People aren't commonly aware of this—unless they're avid readers—but in the publishing industry, it's standard for new releases to come out on Tuesdays. Closing on new release day was off the table. I kept the bookstore open for half a day on Tuesdays simply so Head Rock Harbor readers could get any highly anticipated new releases the day they dropped.

It was possible that I could close the store on Mondays and have Sundays and Mondays off—thus, achieve my 2-day weekend goal. However, I'd always felt that being closed on Sundays was a bad idea. A lot of people love to shop on Sundays, especially after church and lunch. With their bellies full of comfort food and their hearts filled with the Lord, leisurely shopping that led to more purchases than planned was common.

Then again, I always hated dealing with the church crowd. Righteous spill over from the sermon they'd heard that morning made some of them absolutely unbearable.

Quickly, I decided that I would plan to close the shop on Sundays and Mondays. Between Tuesday and Saturday, I'd keep the store open from nine in the morning until seven at night. Except for an hour for lunch, of course. I'd have to put up notices about the change in hours, and give plenty of notice to my customers, but that was easy enough. Considering my decision, I felt satisfied.

Until I realized that my distraction from thinking about Carter Nelson and Jeremy was gone.

Blowing out a frustrated breath, I locked eyes with Rattlesnatches. He blinked lazily up at me from his spot on the kitchen floor next to the table.

"Want to go for a walk?" I asked.

Lazily, after an aloof yawn, Rattlesnatches rose to sit on his haunches and stared up at me. He blinked both eyes once.

I was taking that as a "yes."

Together, we left our apartment and descended the stairs to the store below. At the front door, I slid on a light jacket and a beanie from the coat rack. I retrieved Rattlesnatches' halter and leash from the hook by the door and knelt down to slide it over his lithe body and secure all of the straps. He waited patiently as I prepared him and then grabbed my wallet and keys.

A minute later, we were standing outside of the bookstore as I locked the door securely behind us. The sun was three-quarters of the way through the sky, working its way to the western horizon as we set out on our walk. Instead of heading north towards the bluff, where we'd likely run into less people, we headed south. Though I usually liked to avoid people when walking Rattlesnatches since everyone wanted us to stop so he could be petted, I had a destination in mind. Unfortunately, that destination meant we had to walk through town.

However, with the time approaching the dinner hour, our short walk across downtown resulted in few interruptions. Eventually, we found ourselves nearing Harper's. To avoid anyone in the parking lot or hanging out around outside of my mother's restaurant, we took a wide berth around the building. Going around the south side of the building to catch the trail that ended—or began, depending on how you looked at it—at the east side of the building helped us to avoid people.

Rattlesnatches pranced ahead of me, curiously looking this way and that, checking out the scenery he so rarely got to enjoy. We walked the dirt trail away from Harper's and around the trailer park's north side, around the east side, and down the south side. The sun was dipping lower in the sky, threatening visibility as dusk settled around Head Rock Harbor. When we got to Wilford Street, which cut across the trail before it led into the woods, I decided our walk was over.

Carrying on into the woods when the sun was minutes away from disappearing was a bad idea. Likely, a stroll along the path through the woods would be safe. However, with a small animal that would look like an amuse-bouche to all sorts of woodland creatures, a walk along the trail at night was not advisable.

I gave Rattlesnatches lead a gentle, steady tug as he approached the asphalt of Wilford Street, letting him know our trip had come to an end. He obeyed, turning immediately to head back down the trail in the direction we had come. I followed along, letting him dutifully lead the way back towards the trailer park. As we walked, I wondered why I'd bothered taking a stroll along the trail where Carter Nelson's watch had been found. It had been a whim. What had I actually expected of the walk? That I would discover some profound clue or evidence the police had completely missed?

Snorting derisively at myself, I continued to follow Rattlesnatches' loping gait, picking up my pace to match his. Rattlesnatches, seemingly stimulated by something only he could see, bounced excitedly for several yards before stopping abruptly in the middle of the path. Darkness was creeping in around us as the sun had already set, but his keen kitty eyes had spotted something of interest in the dirt of the path.

With nighttime settling in around us, I attempted to walk past Rattlesnatches, tugging on his leash gently as I did so, hoping to spur him back into action. However, he wasn't to be distracted from whatever had taken his interest. Even as I walked until I had run out of leash and I was left standing a few yards up the trail, looking back at him with annoyance, he stared down at the trail, ignoring me.

"Let's go," I said.

Rattlesnatches ignored me.

"Rattlesnatches," I said again. "Let's go. It's getting dark. Do you want to be coyote or bobcat nom noms?"

Finally, he looked up at me, his coppery eyes twinkling in the gloom.

"*Mew.*"

Of course, I thought, *mew*. That explains everything. Huffing, I walked those few yards back over to Rattlesnatches, ready to entertain his curiosity so that we could finally go home. As I approached, his head turned back down to the ground beneath his feet, and he stared. I crouched down next to him, prepared to admonish him for keeping us out after dark longer than necessary. However, as I knelt, I caught the glimmer of pearlescence at Rattlesnatches' feet.

Quizzically, I tilted my head to the side as my cat rolled his head to stare up at me and mewl once again. Reaching down, I put fingers to the tiny, shiny object on the path and plucked it out of the dirt with my index finger and thumb. Swiping my thumb over the hard, round object, I brought it up, hoping that the dim yellowish-orange light from the sodium lights around the trailer park would help me to examine it.

Rattlesnatches mewled again as I observed the small piece of plastic. I gave it another rub with my thumb and blew violently against it to remove any remaining dirt. Then I tilted it around in my fingers to try and catch enough light to figure out what I was looking at there in the middle of the trail. When I saw the four little holes in the middle of the round object, I realized what Rattlesnatches had found.

A button.

Chapter Twelve

Typically, I don't take my cat into restaurants. Also typical, my mother doesn't allow pets into her restaurant unless they're service animals. Since Rattlesnatches was using his best manners and resting quietly like a gentleman in the booth seat next to me, Deb chose to overlook my odd choice in dinner companion. At least for one evening. Since several other diners—townies who knew me—stopped by the booth to scratch Rattlesnatches behind the ears, it would have looked cruel of her to kick us out.

After our walk along the trail and Rattlesnatches finding his little button token, I didn't want to walk back to the bookstore before stopping for dinner. I decided to sneak Rattlesnatches into the restaurant with me. By "sneak in," I mean that I walked into Harper's with him tucked under my arm like a purse. Deb immediately scowled at the sight of us, but one innocent "*meow*" from Rattlesnatches as he dangled helpless from the crook of my arm changed her mind. Deb flicked a finger towards the back booth in the corner, shaking her head as the two of us made our way to our seat.

As I sat patiently, waiting for my order to be taken, Rattlesnatches twisted his head back and forth, taking in the sights around him. He seemed to know that we were already breaking a rule, as he kept himself low in the booth, his head barely peeking over the table. Discretion is a rule of thumb in our household—two-legged or four-legged family members alike. Well…we like to pretend we know how to behave, at least.

"I'm not bringing out a saucer of milk if you've got yourself thinking that," Deb said as she approached the booth.

"Cats shouldn't have cow's milk. Anyway, I'll feed him when I get home," I replied, speaking louder than normal to be heard over the other diners in the restaurant. "We were out walking and I didn't want to take him home before I fed myself. That's all."

"Mmhm." Deb shook her head. "The usual?"

"Yes, please." I smiled widely up at my mother.

She took a moment to stare down at Rattlesnatches, her face blank as she took in my cat sitting in the booth next to me. When Rattlesnatches realized he was being watched, he turned his head lazily to look up at Deb. For a moment, the two of them stared blankly at each other. Finally, Rattlesnatches issued a disinterested "meow," blinked his eyes, and laid back down on the booth seat, stretching out lazily.

Deb shook her head.

"I'll see if Beau can chop up a little catfish for him." Deb huffed and then turned on her heels without another word.

I smiled after my mother. Deb wasn't a bad person. Simply cranky. I was glad I hadn't mentioned to her that I had planned to sneak small pieces of cheesesteak meat to Rattlesnatches over dinner.

Once I was alone, I pulled the button from my hip pocket. The diners around me carried on with their raucous dinnertime conversations and the folks over in the bar who were playing pool and dancing continued with their shenanigans. I sank back into the red vinyl booth and held the button under the soft glow of the faux Tiffany lamp hung over the table.

Even in the soft lighting of the restaurant, the black and tan button's pearlescence was apparent. Frowning and causing my brow to furrow deeply, I stared at the plastic circle. Though finding a button randomly on a trail was not all that significant, it made my gray matter wiggle. Rattlesnatches had found the object interesting. He rarely found objects interesting unless he could play with them, eat them, or there was something about the object that was unapparent to human eyes.

He was a strange cat. But his instincts were excellent.

Something about the button seemed familiar. Which is an odd thing to think about a button.

A loud metallic clatter at the next table over startled me out of my daydream. When I looked over at the family seated a few yards away, the father was leaning down to pick up his fork he'd dropped on the ground. He gave me an embarrassed, apologetic look and I grinned back at him. When I looked back at the button, my train of thought was gone, so I slipped the small plastic disc back into my pocket.

For a small town, businesses in Head Rock Harbor do fair business. Especially the restaurants and other establishments that sell prepared food items. If there's one thing the people of Head Rock Harbor love—it's not having to cook for themselves. With the reasonable prices at Harper's and Munchies, it's not uncommon for most people in town to eat out for dinner at least three times a week. Even with the current state of the economy and inflation, You could get a cheesesteak and one side at Harper's for under ten bucks. The tenderloin lunch at Munchies would run you around eight dollars.

So, when I looked around Harper's and found it suddenly full, I was not surprised. It was well into the dinner hour and the citizens of Head Rock Harbor needed to fill their bellies. The main draw of Harper's for dinner—as opposed to the more upscale The Dock on the river—was that Harper's had a bar, a pool table, and music. Even though dinner was still in full swing, the bar was doing respectable business. At least a dozen people were in the room on the other side of the building, sipping simple cocktails and beers, choosing songs on the jukebox, and challenging each other to games of pool.

Though it was nothing fancy, Harper's was clean and appealing. Deb ran a tight ship around her restaurant and bar. The wood floors were scuffed and gouged from years of use—but they were clean enough to eat dinner off of if you so choose. The hanging faux Tiffany lamps were a bit gaudy, but you'd be hard pressed to find a bit of dust on them. Some of the booth seats had seen better days—and had been temporarily repaired with duct tape—and all of the tables and chairs had been through the ringer. But all of the blinds on the windows were in good order, functioning, and free of grime.

The kitchen was spotless, cleaned from top to bottom each night before closing. You wouldn't find spots on your cups, plates, and silverware. The salt and pepper shakers, ketchup and mustard bottles, Tabasco sauce, and other condiments left on the tables were always wiped clean of grease and grime. The menus were always wiped clean, and if found damaged, quickly replaced. Basically, if you could deal with the sometimes-rowdy crowd—a fist being thrown at eleven o'clock on a Saturday night was not rare—you could have a good time and a good affordable meal.

When Deb delivered my cheesesteak, rings, and coleslaw—and a small plate of chopped catfish for Rattlesnatches—she didn't linger. There were too many fresh diners waiting to have their orders taken. I silently thanked whatever entity floats above for that small kindness. Fortunately, that meant I could start my meal in peace. I set the small saucer of catfish on the booth seat in front of Rattlesnatches and he immediately began to chow down.

As hungry as my cat, I immediately dug into my cheesesteak, devouring it like a starving man, slurping up large mouthfuls of soda between bites. Though I'd had a hearty lunch at Munchies, I felt like I hadn't eaten since breakfast. Of course, being asked by your detective friend to get involved in the investigation of a maybe-not-suicide can really do a number on a guy. It hits you right in the appetite bone.

Before I knew it, my cheesesteak was gone. My soda cup was empty, most of the ice still sparkling in the glass. And only two rings remained on my plate. Ordering dessert became the debate between the angel and devil in my brain. I was still a little hungry, but I had really been trying to eat less sweets. My diet was awful to begin with, so cutting out some of the garbage was a good idea. Finally, I settled on the decision that I wouldn't make a decision. I'd order dessert *if it felt right.* If the time came and it simply seemed necessary, so be it.

"You seen the paper?" I jumped when Deb set a fresh cup of soda next to my plate and grabbed my empty cup. "Just this mornin'?"

"The paper?" I asked dumbly.

"The newspaper, genius," Deb said with a chuckle. "*The Herald.* Whatever you want to call it, fancy pants."

I rolled my eyes and plucked one of the two remaining onion rings from my plate. Rolling my hand to indicate she should continue, I looked up at Deb and bit into the onion ring.

"Says you're going to be in charge of organizing the first ever Head Rock Harbor Pride," Deb said.

Scowling, I stuffed the rest of the ring in my mouth and chewed aggressively.

"What?" Deb asked.

"I literally," I mumbled, then realized my mouth was full, chewed, and swallowed before continuing, "just talked to Linda about that this morning. How's it in *today's* paper?"

Deb shrugged and crossed her arms over her chest.

"I'm guessing she told them to print without confirming." Deb grinned.

"I should have said no."

"Well," Deb asked, "you need help?"

Immediately, my brain began to spin with polite ways to tell my mother that having her help me plan the Pride event would be akin to wiping with sandpaper. Unfortunately, with a full belly, my brain wasn't working as quickly as I liked.

So, I stuffed the other onion ring in my mouth and chewed it thoughtfully as I stared up at my mother.

Rolling her eyes, Deb took my plate from the table in her other hand. Quickly, I grabbed the saucer—now clear of catfish—and laid it atop the dinner plate in her hand. Though she should have known better than to think I'd want to partner up on the Pride event planning, Deb had asked anyway. And by the current look on her face, I could tell she had already chastised herself mentally for bothering to ask.

"Loud and clear, turd," Deb said. "I didn't want to help you anyway."

"I didn't say anything."

"You ain't got to." Deb huffed. "Most boys would be happy their mother was so accepting and supportive. Not you, though."

So...here we are again, I thought to myself.

Deb was going to launch into her speech about how she was a card-carrying PFLAG mother and I should be pleased.

I was pleased. Though I'd never seen the actual card.

I simply didn't want to organize a Pride event with her. Having to cooperate with and compromise on ideas with my mother was unappealing. I'd done that enough in my childhood and teen years. Even when I'd moved out in my mid-teens to live with my aunt, there was never a point Deb had ever been fully extricated from my life. Now, as a grown man, there were parts of my life that I wanted to be my own.

A gay man organizing a Pride event—that I didn't really want to organize to begin with—was one of those parts. And it had nothing to do with the fact that if Deb was involved it would look like every rainbow item from a craft store had puked on Head Rock Harbor. No. I wasn't thinking that

Deb's level of taste was questionable. I simply wanted to be a grown gay man organizing the event on my own.

Honestly.

It suddenly occurred to me that Deb had been talking— about being a proud mother, of course—and I had tuned out. I was staring through glazed eyes at her, but I wasn't hearing a single word coming from her mouth as she snarled down at me. When I finally forced myself back into the here and now, she was ending her rant.

"...and that's why you need to find a boyfriend," Deb said, ending her rant with a flourish.

I blinked up at her.

"You didn't hear a word I said, did you?" She sighed.

Thinking quickly, I reached down and laid a hand over Rattlesnatches' head, covering his ears.

"Not in front of the children, mother," I said, admonishing her. "We can't fight in front of the children!"

Deb rolled her eyes. I was loading another quip into the chamber, a grin forming on my face for my delivery, when I noticed the front door of Harper's open. Though it took a second, I quickly recognized the young man coming through the door. Colton Nelson—Carter Nelson's son—shuffled into Harper's, his eyes down, his head hung. Rattlesnatches' head popped up over the table, then he sunk back in the seat.

Narrowing my eyes, I stared at Colton as he looked around Harper's furtively, then slunk into the bar area. With Deb blocking my view, I lost sight of him once he was in the bar. Deb looked over her shoulder at what had obviously gotten my attention. When she turned back to face me, she was frowning disapprovingly. With a sigh, she set my plate and cup back on the table, then slid into the booth across from me.

"Jackson," she said, "what are you looking at?"

"Nothing." I shrugged, feigning innocence.

Deb considered me for a moment.

"You leave that boy alone. And Myrna and them other boys," Deb said. "You don't need to get involved in that mess."

"What mess?" I perked up, wondering if Deb had heard anything suspicious about Carter Nelson, his death, or his family. "What have you heard?"

Rolling her eyes, Deb waved an exhausted hand at me.

"This is what I'm talkin' about," she said. "That man killed himself and the family is mourning. They don't need anyone bothering them with questions and suspicions. Let him rest in peace and let the family get over it. He isn't even buried yet, for crying out loud."

I frowned. "When's the funeral?"

Deb sighed. "Sunday."

"Seems quick. All things considered." My brow furrowed as I considered Carter Nelson's death.

"You're still doing it!" Deb jabbed an accusatory finger at me. "There's nothing suspicious about a man dying on a Sunday and being buried the following Sunday. It happens all the time."

"Not when a supposed suicide is the cause of death," I said. "A *violent* supposed suicide."

"You say. But you're wrong."

"What if I'm not?"

"You listen here," Deb sat forward, folding her hands atop the table between us. "Imagine that you are right.

Imagine that someone else killed Carter Nelson. He didn't shoot himself. Someone else did it. Right?"

I nodded.

"Do you want to have that person knowing that you're trying to find them?" Deb asked. "Wouldn't that be dangerous? Maybe they'd want to come find you next so you can't find evidence linking them to the crime? You ever think about that?"

I started to respond, but Deb wasn't finished.

"You'd be putting a target right on your back, Jackson," she said, continuing. "Also, if there's a murderer out there, they've killed one person. No one else has died. So, this was a personal issue. This isn't some maniac going around killin' a bunch of people in town and *you gotta find 'em before they strike again.*"

Again, I opened my mouth, but Deb didn't pause.

"If there's a murderer, let the cops handle it, for goodness' sake," Deb said. "And if they don't, that's not your problem. That's for the family's and the cops' conscience. Not *you.*"

"But—"

"And now let's imagine you're wrong," Deb said. "Carter Nelson shot himself and you're acting a fool over nothing. It's tragic—but it's not anything worth investigating. *Because* you'll be causing more harm to his family and his memory. You're just stirring up hurt and pain when that man should be allowed to rest and his family should get to mourn and pick up the pieces."

I stared at her.

"You hear me?" she finally indicated it was my turn to speak.

"Loud and clear," I responded.

She watched me for a moment.

"But you ain't gonna listen, are you?" she sighed, flopping back in the booth.

"Probably not, no," I said.

Deb hauled herself out of the booth across from me. Diligently, she collected my plates and empty cup once again, and stared down at me. Rattlesnatches and I stared up at her, innocent looks on our faces.

"You get shot—don't come cryin' to me," Deb said, started to walk away, then turned back to me. "And if you piss off the Nelsons and they come after you, don't expect me to defend you!"

With that, Deb turned and left in a huff. I looked down at Rattlesnatches. He sat there on his haunches, looking up at me, and blinked slowly. Obviously, he was as unimpressed with Deb's dramatics as I was. Whether I was right or wrong, there *was* something fishy about Carter's death. Jeremy had asked me to look into it. Even if I didn't owe it to Carter to figure out what had actually happened at the campsite when he died, I owed my friend.

That's what I was going to keep telling myself.

Before I could talk myself out of it, I took a long sip of my soda, then slid out of the booth. I lifted Rattlesnatches and tucked him into the crook of my arm. Together, we walked over to the bar, my soda cup in hand. I sipped on it diligently, trying to finish it before I got to the bar. As I stepped up to speak to Cleo in the bright and loud bar area, the cup was nothing but ice and I was nearly out of breath from chugging the drink.

"Hey!" I announced loudly to be heard over the other patrons. "Cleo!"

Cleo St. Clair, gorgeous in all black and faux biker gear—like always—looked up at me from the draft beer she was pouring expertly from the tap.

"Hey, Jackson!" she replied with a grin. "You already eat?"

"Yeah." I said. "I just wanted to leave my glass here so Deb doesn't accuse me of not cleaning up after myself.

Cleo gave a full-throated laugh as she finished the beer and shoved it across the bar to a waiting man. He slid her a few ones and she quickly pocketed them. A bartender, cabaret performer, and sometimes stripper—Cleo was not unfamiliar with tipping culture. She knew not to leave bills sitting out for sticky hands. She reached across the bar and took the cup from me, jiggled it at me and winked.

"Thanks!"

"Thank you," I said. "Have a good night."

"You too, Jackson," she replied brightly before dumping the ice in the sink and then turning to put my cup in the dirty dishes tub.

Bringing my empty cup to Cleo had served two purposes. Deb actually would have complained about me leaving my cup at the table instead of dealing with it myself. Especially after my free meal and her clearing away my other dishes. I wanted to avoid that issue. That part was true. However, I had also needed a reason to venture into the bar. One that seemed perfectly innocent and believable.

The second reason for venturing into the bar was easily spotted a few barstools away from where I was standing. Fortunately, most of the bar patrons were not sitting at the bar, shooting the breeze. They were playing pool, dancing, flirting, or sitting at the bar tables around the perimeter of the room. I had a clear shot to Colton Nelson—and my perfectly believable excuse to be in the bar gave me opportunity.

Still cradling Rattlesnatches as his head turned back and forth, taking in the scene, I edged down the bar, until I was next to Colton. His head was down, looking into the froth of an already half-empty beer. For a moment, I reconsidered talking to him. He looked as though he had come to Harper's specifically to drown his sorrows, which was understandable, all things considered. I desperately wanted to tell him that sorrows were Olympic swimmers. However, I didn't feel it would be welcome so soon after his father's death. Instead, I stuck to my original plan.

"Well, we're just running into each other all over the place," I said brightly.

Colton, slightly jostled by my sudden appearance, wobbled on his barstool. I gave a polite chuckle as he braced himself against the bar and turned to look up at me. He gave me a sheepish, though sad, smile.

"Oh," he said after a moment, "yeah. You're that guy...from Munchies?"

"Jackson Harper," I said, holding my hand out.

"Colton Nelson." He took my hand and gave it a shake. "But...you know that. Everyone knows that. Now."

I gave him an understanding smile as he turned back to stare down into his beer.

"You holding up okay?" I asked.

He shrugged slightly.

"Doing my best," he sighed, staring at his beer. "If this is *best.*"

I patted him on the back, his Carhartt button up rough under my hand.

"We all do what we gotta do to get by sometimes," I said.

He nodded. "Yeah. I mean, I know it's weird...coming here...all things considered. Especially, you know, since Dad...well, you know."

I listened. People talk more—and give more information—if you simply listen.

"He died instead of coming here," Colton said, finally. "I just wish he hadn't left us that night. You know? He could have just come here. He'd still be alive. I know he was mad at me, but going back to the campsite and...it just doesn't feel right. He should have been here with us."

"He left you?" I couldn't help but ask.

Colton, as though suddenly realizing I was still there, turned his head and stared up at me, shocked. At first, I thought maybe I had ruined my chances of finding out more details about the night Carter died, but Colton's expression finally relaxed.

"Yeah," he said. "He was going to walk up here with us. Then he got mad. I'm...I'm not really supposed to be drinking? But I just wanted to hang out with my cousins. Have some fun. You know? Dad got mad. We were almost here and he threw a fit when he found out I planned to do a little drinking. Man. *Red in the face* mad. I shouldn't have screamed back at him. I should've just said, *okay, I won't drink. Not if you come with us.* He'd still be alive. He wouldn't have done what he did."

I stared at the side of Colton's face as he turned back to his beer.

"But I had to be a jerk and leave him there on the trail. I couldn't swallow my pride, man. You know? I had to be a big shot for my cousins. Not take my old man's crap. And he's dead. Nothing fixes that."

Colton lifted the beer to his lips and began a long slug of the amber liquid. As he drank, my eyes drifted to his shirt. Tan and black pearlescent buttons caught my eye and I found myself staring. Without thinking twice, I scanned the shirt from top to button, looking for a gap in the buttons. Colton finished the beer in the mug and tapped it on the counter, getting Cleo's attention. Dutifully, she came over and grabbed the mug with a sympathetic smile.

When Colton turned back to look at me, I was staring at the bottom of his shirt. When he saw me staring, his expression turned quizzical.

"Uh," he said, "you okay?"

Snapping out of my daze, I lifted my eyes to look at Colton.

"Sorry," I said quickly, hoping he hadn't assumed I was checking him out. "Yeah. I'm good."

I lifted the arm holding Rattlesnatches. Colton, having not noticed the cat in my arm before, grew wide-eyed at the sight of the Abyssinian.

"I gotta get my cat home," I said. "Again, I'm sorry about your loss. Tell Myrna and your cousins the same again for me."

Colton gave me a nod as Cleo set a full mug in front of him, and I turned on my heels. As fast as I could without power walking, I exited the bar and dipped out of Harper's

Bar, Grill, Bait & Tackle. Once in the parking lot, I found my breath hitched in my throat.

Colton's shirt wasn't missing any buttons.

But I now knew why the little plastic disk seemed so familiar when I examined it.

Carhartt was popular in Head Rock Harbor—as it was in many small, country towns, particularly where cold weather was common. Lots of button ups. Lots of buttons. Many looking exactly like the one residing in my pocket.

As I walked through the streets back to the bookstore, I wondered what Carter Nelson had been wearing the night he died. What had the cousins been wearing? Colton? Who might be missing a button?

And did a missing button mean anything at all?

Chapter Thirteen

Jeremy wasn't impressed with my evidence. He said so via text.

When I got home from Harper's after finding the button and examining Colton Nelson's shirt—*maybe too closely*— I had texted Jeremy. I laid out the walk with Rattlesnatches, the button, talking to Colton—everything. Ultimately, he decided that a random button found on a trail walked by thousands of people yearly was not evidence of anything.

I didn't like it when Jeremy was rational.

So, when I rolled out of bed on Thursday morning, I found myself with a choice to make. Quickly showering and getting ready for the day, I stuffed some breakfast down my gullet, fed Rattlesnatches, and dressed for the day. Instead of opening the shop for the day, I made sure the "Closed" sign was displayed prominently in the front window of the shop, and left the shop through the back, hopping into the Beetle.

I sat in the car, waiting on the heater to kick in—a Herculean task for a 30-year-old vehicle—as I pulled up Google on my phone. A few searches later, I found out that the morgue and forensics department for Head Rock Harbor weren't actually at the police department. They were both located at the Head Rock Harbor Regional Hospital out on the highway. The hospital was a fancier, updated building that had been built when the old hospital had been razed five years earlier. When the hospital and morgue moved, the decision had been made to use the additional space for the forensics department.

Being able to locate that information online instead of asking Jeremy was a godsend. If I'd asked Jeremy about the forensics department and the morgue, I'm not certain how he would have responded. Going out to the woods and looking around, talking to people and being a nuisance—that was acceptable. Poking my nose in official places where cops and city officials worked might have been pushing the limits.

Jeremy wanted my help, but he didn't want me garnering attention.

It was best if I went rogue.

Once the Beetle no longer felt like an icebox on an early Iowa spring morning, I puttered out of the alley behind the bookstore and headed out to the highway. By mid-afternoon, a drive out to the hospital with the windows down might have been pleasurable. However, early Iowa spring mornings are notoriously frosty. Even if the sun is out and shining all day long, a heater is required in the morning and at night. The window of warm hours during early spring is small.

The new hospital didn't have the same charm as the old one in town. Once a stately brick and stone building, reminiscent of a Queen Anne-style estate, served our town's medical needs. Now, an industrial brick, metal, and glass building sat out on the highway, LED lights illuminating the cold exterior. Acres of concrete encircled the building for the cars of the plethora of visitors from Head Rock Harbor and nearby small towns.

I hated to think of a hospital—an essential building and service to a community—as an eyesore, but the place simply wasn't cute. Function over aesthetics, I supposed. Even if I didn't like the way the hospital looked, plunked out by itself in the middle of nowhere, it served its purpose. Fortunately, it seemed like Mayor Wagner and the City Council were relegating all new builds to the outskirts of town and the highway. For the time being, downtown Head Rock Harbor was going to retain its smalltown charm.

Parking my car near the main entrance, I entered the hospital through the revolving glass door. It took a stop at three different information desks on the first floor before I was given helpful information, but I finally found the morgue. As it had been in the old hospital, the basement of the new hospital was dark, dreary, and a bit creepy. I never thought that Hell might be illuminated by greenish-yellow fluorescent lighting, but the hospital basement had me considering the possibility.

It had taken a short elevator ride down one floor and a brief walk down an eerie unoccupied hallway to find the morgue. Fortunately, the door to the forensics department was directly next to the morgue, so a second search wasn't needed. Not knowing what else to do, I knocked on the door to the morgue. After several minutes, and no answer after a few additional knocks, I gave up. I stepped down to the forensics department door and gave it a knock.

A moment later, the door swung inwards, and I wasn't surprised to find Deacon Davis staring out at me from the brightly lit room. Deacon, however, was shocked to find me at his door. He was covered head-to-toe in a white papery jumpsuit of some kind. Though the sides of his head had been shaved down considerably, the thick strip of long blond hair atop his head had been pulled back into a man bun of sorts. His hand holding the door was clad in a purple nitrile glove.

"Jackson?" he asked, reaching up to remove his goggles.

He suddenly seemed to remember he was wearing—*possibly*—contaminated gloves, and stopped himself.

"Hey...Deacon," I responded. "How are you?"

I don't know what I'd expected when I'd knocked on the door, but I'd hoped someone I didn't know would answer. More specifically, I'd hoped someone who didn't know anything about my involvement in finding Carter Nelson's body would have answered the door. Then again, Head Rock Harbor didn't need a huge forensics team. It was likely that Deacon was the sole employee.

"I'm...good," he answered, suspicion lacing his tone. "What's up? You get lost?"

"Well—"

"No one ever comes down here," Deacon said.

He stuck his head out and glanced up and down the hallway before leaning back and looking at me again.

"It's *creepy*." He held both purple gloved hands up and wiggled his fingers at me.

Laughing, I said, "I wanted to ask a favor."

Deacon gave me a sideways smile and examined me for a moment, then stepped back, holding the door wide for me. He swung an arm grandly, inviting me inside.

"Enter my lair," he said.

Chuckling, since rolling my eyes would not endear me to Deacon, I stepped into the room. My eyes were immediately assaulted by the bright lighting, sterile white walls, steel surfaces, and the haze of chemicals I couldn't name. My nose twitched at the smells and I had the sudden urge to sneeze.

"I was just finishing up some urine and blood samples," Deacon said, stepping around me to venture further into the room towards a steel worktable. "What's the favor?"

"Well," I said, reaching up to scratch my nose, "as you know, I was one of the people who found Carter Nelson's body. Out in Wilford Woods?"

"Yep," Deacon nodded as he began fiddling with what looked like stoppered test tubes on the table. "Forest green Mack Weldons."

"I—what?"

"You were wearing forest green Mack Weldon boxer briefs when I did my collection," Deacon turned his head to me to smile. "I haven't forgotten you, Jackson. Even without the underwear memory, it's not like it's easy to forget someone in Head Rock Harbor. There's, what? Two dozen citizens?"

Nervously, I laughed. What he'd said was actually funny, but him remembering me in my underwear was embarrassing.

"Yeah," I said, "well, I wanted to know where his body is. Is it in the morgue?"

Deacon lost interest in his test tubes and turned to me, leaning against the table casually.

"Building a Frankenstein's monster?"

"No," I shook my head. "I want to look at the clothes he was wearing."

"Need inspiration for your next hunter cosplay?"

I frowned at him.

"Why?" Deacon asked, understandably suspicious. "You're not a police officer. You're not family. Why do you need to see his clothes?"

For a moment, I contemplated throwing Jeremy under the bus. Admit that he'd asked me to help him look into Carter Nelson's death. However, I wasn't certain what Deacon would do with that information. He seemed like a nice enough guy, but I didn't know if he'd feel compelled to report me directly to Chief Bucksworth. However, I hadn't planned a plausible enough lie before driving out to the hospital. First rule of nosing around—have a good lie ready.

"The truth?" I asked.

"It would be appreciated," Deacon said with a nod.

"I'm helping someone look into his death," I said. "I don't want to give too much information so that I don't get anyone else in trouble. But I just want to see if the shirt he died in is missing a button."

Deacon was unfazed.

"He shot himself in the chest," he said blandly. "I'm certain a button or two might be missing."

"Do you really think he shot himself?" I found myself blurting out the question.

Deacon stared at me.

"I mean," I stammered, "doesn't it...seem odd to you? The circumstances around his death?"

He said nothing.

"That's...that's why I'm looking into it. I don't want to bother the family any more than necessary. So...I thought I'd see if I could learn anything here. I simply want to make sure that if he didn't commit suicide that something is done about it. Please?"

Deacon continued to stare at me for several moments longer, then finally, with a sigh, he began to remove his gloves. I watched as he meticulously removed the gloves and dumped them into a hazardous waste container. He then washed his hands thoroughly at the sink before removing his googles and jumpsuit. Which then required another handwashing. I stood there and waited as Deacon removed potentially hazardous materials from his body.

He could have been preparing to call security or the police. And I stood there stupidly. However, with no other option than to wait and see what he would do, I said nothing and waited.

"So," Deacon began once he dried his hands for the last time, his back to me as he stood at the sink, "let me show you something."

"Okay?"

"And you tell me what you think about it," Deacon continued. "If you see the problem, I'll let you see his clothes."

I breathed out. "Okay. Deal."

Deacon turned to me with a twinkle in his eye.

"You're lucky," he said. "The funeral home is picking up his body this afternoon. They'd likely take the clothes and burn them. Or leave them for us to dispose of later. Because the families usually don't want clothes from violent deaths back. Good timing, Jackson."

I simply smiled and followed him as he led me out of the forensics department. My eyes practically sang with relief once we stepped out into the dark hallway. Leading me down to the morgue, Deacon swiped his badge along a plate next to the door, and an electronic buzz, followed by a click, granted us access to the room.

Following him into the room, he flicked on lights that were considerably kinder to the eyes than those in the lab. The two of us traversed the room over to the wall of freezers where bodies were kept. The sudden realization of what I was about to endure struck me and I wasn't sure I wanted to go along with Deacon's deal. However, I knew that if I wanted any chance to see Carter's clothes before they were likely destroyed, I had to see Carter's body, too.

"You're not squeamish, are you?" Deacon asked as we approached one of the freezers. "If you'll likely puke, I can't have that."

I shook my head. "I've already seen him. Dead, I mean."

Deacon did a head cock-like nod.

"Seeing them freshly dead and seeing them after they've been dissected and poked and prodded is different," Deacon said, warning me.

"I'll be fine," I said.

Deacon shrugged, and with a jerk of the freezer handle, the door popped open. A blast of cold air and a hazy billow of air gusted out of the coffin-sized hole in the wall. He jerked on the handle for the tray and out came Carter Nelson. Well, Carter Nelson encased in a body bag. Deacon said nothing as the two of us moved to stand on either side of the tray and he pulled the zipper down on the bag.

"If you feel sick, turn the other way. Don't puke on my corpse." Deacon warned me again.

I nodded, but kept my mouth shut in case.

Then Carter Nelson's face and upper chest were exposed. Fortunately, his eyes were not open. I don't know if I could have handled that. Of course, it was probably routine to make sure corpse's eyes were closed before storing them. That's the logic my mind worked out, anyway. Deacon waved a hand over the body.

"So," Deacon said, "show me you deserve to see his clothes."

Frowning, my brow like a crevice, I glanced at Deacon. He stared at me and motioned at Carter's body. What he expected me to find simply by looking at Carter's face and chest, I was unsure. However, there had to be something obvious if Deacon expected me to figure it out with such a small amount of the body exposed.

I stared down at Carter's blotchy face and blotchy and bruised upper chest, glad that Deacon hadn't unzipped the bag enough to expose the wound in his chest. Looking into the shotgun blast hole—or, even more likely—the incisions from an autopsy, was not ideal. I was willing to look at Carter's body, but blood and guts were not preferable.

"You okay?" Deacon asked.

I nodded as I stared down at Carter. I hadn't noticed all of the bruising and blotches when Sawyer and I had found him in the woods. Then again, the find was a surprise, and staring at a dead body wasn't something I found pleasurable.

"The funeral home has its work cut out for it," I sighed.

Deacon made an agreeable sound with his throat.

Carter Nelson, a reasonably handsome man in life, was anything but attractive in death. A bit bloated, blotchy, bruised, and cyanotic, he wasn't going to find any matches on a dating site anytime soon. The funeral home was going to have to cake on makeup to make him presentable for an open casket funeral. Of course, maybe the Nelsons had decided on closed casket. I hadn't asked, and I didn't care to know. But I knew the family wouldn't want to see the blotchiness and bruising.

And then it struck me.

"*He died face down,*" I said, whispering to myself.

"I'm sorry?" Deacon asked quickly.

I stared down at Carter's face a moment longer, then looked up at Deacon.

"He...Carter. He died face down," I said again, louder. "Post-mortem lividity. The blotches. Discoloration. The blood settled on this side of his body. If he shot himself while lying on his back—or shot himself and fell onto his back as we found him—those blotches wouldn't be there. They'd be on his backside. He died faced down. Someone turned him over after he was dead for a while. The post mortem lividity...he must have been dead at least a few hours before he was turned. Right?"

Deacon simply smiled at me.

"But," I said, turning my attention back to Carter's body, "that abrasion on his chin and his chest. Those aren't from livor mortis. Those are from some type of impact. He fell, hitting his chin and chest. But before his blood stopped pumping. He had a fall—*and then he died.*"

"Correct," Deacon said. "Well, that's my theory."

"Did you tell Jeremy?" I looked up at him quickly.

Deacon shrugged. "The post-mortem lividity and bruising are notated in the forensic notes and the autopsy notes from the ME. But I'm new here. I don't try to solve the cops' crimes for them."

I snorted, amused. "Fair enough."

Deacon began to zip the body bag up.

"So," I asked urgently, "it's safe to say that this wasn't suicide. Right? He died from a fall. Probably."

Deacon, irritatingly, shrugged again.

"Possible," he said. "I can't say for sure. He was definitely shot. Barely missed his heart. Bisected his aorta. I'm not a medical examiner, either. However, it's worth investigating why he obviously died on his stomach but he was found on his back. Right? That suggests, bare minimum, that someone messed with the body after death."

Morbid as it was, I smiled. Now we were onto something. Jeremy and I weren't completely crazy for feeling something was off about the scene from Sunday morning.

"So," Deacon said, "about those clothes."

"Yeah?" I shook my head to clear my thoughts.

At least until I was alone in my car with silence.

"You don't need to see them. His shirt was missing four buttons. Out of seven. It's notated in the reports."

"Deacon," I said, "thank you."

"Anytime," he said.

"Were they multi-colored and pearlescent? Gray and black?"

He thought about that for a second, then nodded.

"Sounds right."

"Okay," I said. "Thanks again. I've got work to do. Thank you, thank you, thank you, Deacon."

I hurried away from the wall of freezers towards the door leading out of the morgue. My hand had barely touched the handle when Deacon's voice stopped me.

"You know," Deacon said, "after a long day in the lab, I sometimes need a drink."

Turning at the door, still holding the handle, I smiled at him.

"I can imagine dead bodies and their fluids require a beer or two, sure."

He nodded. "Sometimes it's fun to have those beers with someone else. Talk. Get to know each other. That kind of thing?"

Figuring out what Deacon was getting at took me long enough that Jeremy would have been regretting asking for my investigative help.

"Oh."

"If you ever want to get a drink," Deacon shrugged, then reached up to scratch the back of his neck.

It was such a Midwestern guy behavior. The *aw, shucks* scratching of the back of the neck. Typically, I found that sort of thing adorable. On Deacon, I wasn't certain. He was too slight. Too young. But the morgue was definitely too cold to linger in forever.

"How old are you?" I asked, chuckling softly.

"Old enough to legally go for a drink," he said, amused but defensive.

I stared at him.

"Twenty-four," he said.

"You don't look a day over nineteen," I said.

"That is the nicest way I've ever been told to get lost," he smiled ruefully, looking down at his feet. "I mean…are you saying 'no?'"

Thinking about the situation, and what Deacon had done for me, I wasn't certain saying "no" was polite. Even if it was my first instinct. He was an appropriate age, only three years younger than me. And it wasn't as if my romantic prospects in Head Rock Harbor were significant.

"Sure," I said. "A drink sometime would be okay."

Deacon smiled and his eyes were back on me. "Cool. I'll text you."

I nodded. "Thanks again, Deacon."

As I exited the morgue and walked down the hallway to the elevator, my mind raced with the discovery I'd made about Carter Nelson's death. Buttons and blotches filled my head as I considered how to talk to Jeremy about what I'd discovered. Of course, in the corner of my mind, I knew that one day in the near future, Deacon would ask me out for a drink. And I'd go.

We'd end up at Harper's, I was certain.

And I'd never hear the end of questions from my mother.

One problem at a time.

Chapter Fourteen

I slapped my hand on the kitchen bar counter and pulled it away, leaving the buttons behind.

"Four buttons!" I declared.

I'd been waiting on Jeremy's porch after dark when he got home from work, a handful of evidence in my hip pocket. After leaving the hospital and speaking with Deacon over Carter's corpse, I went straight to Wilford Woods. I walked the trail from the back of Harper's to Carter's former campsite at least a dozen times. Meticulously, I searched the ground for any sign of the buttons from Carter's shirt.

The sun inched lazily across the sky as I shuffled slowly back and forth on the trail, eyes wide open for any sign of the missing buttons. I found the second button not far from where Rattlesnatches had found the first one. It was on the other side of the road before heading into the woods. The third button was near the base of a tree leading down the hill into the woods. The fourth—and hardest to find button—was underneath a few leaves I'd nudged out of the way with the toes of my shoes near the campsite.

However, I'd accounted for all of the buttons. On its face, the collection of buttons wouldn't mean much to most people. When one considered that the four buttons were strewn along the route from Harper's to the campsite—or vice versa—questions started to emerge. Why had Carter lost four buttons from his shirt? And why not all in one place? If he had fallen—as the bruise on his chest and chin suggested—one would think the place he fell would be where all the buttons fell off.

The spacing out of the locations of the buttons suggested that they dropped off one by one. Possibly loosened or ripped away from his supposed fall, the buttons had fallen off in different locations. This suggested that *after* he fell, Carter Nelson had gotten up and walked away, losing buttons along his route.

Potentially.

There were other possible explanations.

When I pulled the strip of cloth from his Carhartt shirt from my other pocket and laid it on the counter next to the buttons, I grinned wider. I'd found the piece of cloth, supposedly ripped away from Carter's shirt, on a tree at the base of the hill leading down into the woods. I had to theorize that this was the site of his fall. He had fallen near the tree and the rough bark had ripped away part of his shirt. However, this presented a huge problem. Why were their buttons further behind on the trail, and others further down the trail?

None of it made sense. But it did suggest that there was more going on with Carter Nelson's death than simple suicide.

"Let me read the report," I said with a wide grin.

Jeremy stared down at the buttons and the strip of cloth on the counter, unimpressed.

"Because you found...*buttons?*" He looked up at me, one eyebrow raised.

"Because I found *four buttons* in *four separate locations* on the trail and a strip of his shirt in another location."

"Oh," Jeremy said. "Sure. Yeah. That explains everything."

"The man left pieces of his clothing in several different places, Jeremy," I huffed, exasperated. "Why was he shedding pieces of clothing like tree leaves in autumn? That definitely suggests something odd. And you said if I found something to make you think you're not crazy for suspecting something was off about Carter's death, then—"

"I'd risk bringing you a copy of the report," Jeremy said, finishing my thought.

"This," I waved my hand over the pieces of evidence on the bar counter, "indicates that something was going on that none of us know about. Maybe it's not sinister, but it's something. Something unusual."

Jeremy considered the evidence on his kitchen counter for a moment. I could practically hear the wheels turning in his head as he stared down at the buttons and the strip of cloth.

"I don't know, Jacks. Maybe we're crazy. Maybe the Nelsons were right for getting upset when we arrested Mavis. This is a suicide, whether we like it or not. There's no point in putting an innocent person in jail over it."

Jeremy reached up to rake his fingers through his scraggle of golden curls and scrunched his face up tiredly.

"Okay, okay," I said, realizing his day had probably been long. "Livor mortis."

"What?" Jeremy's head snapped up to look at me.

"Postmortem lividity," I continued. "Carter—those blotches all over the front of him? That's where the blood settled after his death. It's livor mortis, and—"

"I know what livor mortis and postmortem lividity are, Jacks."

"Sorry." I waved him off. "Anyway, Carter died on his stomach. Or, at least, that's where he was very shortly after he died. Livor mortis tells us that from the blotchiness where his blood pooled postmortem. Right?"

Jeremy eyed me.

"So," I said, "we found him on his back. Bare minimum, someone messed with his corpse after his death but before we found him that morning. He had to have been dead for a few hours before they moved his body. *That's something that should tell you that you're not crazy.*"

"How do you know about this?" Jeremy asked, folding his arms over his chest. "Postmortem lividity and livor mortis? But mostly, how do you know what Carter's corpse looks like without his shirt on?"

I grinned awkwardly. Telling Jeremy about my research for the Harrison Garner series was out of the question. Fortunately, I didn't have to come up with a quick, evasive answer.

"Deacon," Jeremy said, shaking his head.

"Don't go trying to get him in trouble," I growled, secretly relieved. "I asked nicely and he—"

"Thought you were cute enough to help, I'm sure," Jeremy grumbled quietly.

"What?"

"Jacks," Jeremy sighed, "you're right. Okay? You're right. These things do point to something strange."

"Thank you." I beamed.

"But you can't just roll up into the hospital and ask Deacon to show you corpses and evidence and—"

"Why not?" I asked. "You basically deputized me. If you can ask me for help, I can ask Deacon for help."

Jeremy frowned at me. He obviously had no argument, so he was simply going to be stubborn.

"He fell before he died, Jeremy," I said, ignoring his angry look. "His chin and chest are abraded. He lost pieces of clothing in multiple places in the woods and along the trail. Maybe we'll find out that him falling frazzled him and knocked something loose upstairs so that he ended up shooting himself—maybe even by accident—but the evidence shows he didn't just shoot himself and fall over dead. End of story."

Jeremy sighed. "Okay."

"Okay?"

"I'll get you the report, Jacks," Jeremy said, doing his best to smile at me.

He earned a return smile, so I gave him one.

"Tomorrow evening after work," Jeremy said. "Meet you here?"

"I'll arrive under the cover of darkness yet again to avoid Marv's wrath." I teased. "Just for you."

Jeremy chuckled. A niggling thought prickled at the corners of my mind. Pictures of Carter on the tray in the morgue flashed through my mind. What my memory could scrounge up from the scene at the campsite when we'd found him.

"Germ?"

"Yeah?" he asked, pulling off his coat and draping it across the bar.

"Suppose Carter did commit suicide by shooting himself in the chest."

Jeremy indicated with a wave of his hand that I should continue.

"He blasts himself in the chest. Shouldn't he have fallen backwards? Isn't that enough to tell you that there's a problem here?"

He stared at me.

"But, after his death, he fell forward. That's why there are blotches on his chest and face from livor mortis. But let's say, by some miracle of physics, he shot himself and fell forward and that explains everything about the livor mortis."

"Okay?"

"With the shot so close to his heart, and having bisected his aorta—according to Deacon—he likely would have lost a lot—*a lot*—of blood through the wound. I don't know that the livor mortis would be as profound as it is."

Jeremy's eyes narrowed as he considered my train of thought.

"I don't remember there being a lot of blood at the scene. The campsite. In fact, it was pretty bloodless for such a violent death."

The two of us stood there in silence for a moment.

"What if…"

Jeremy waited a moment.

"What if *what*, Jacks?" He urged me on, desperately.

I shook my head and chuckled, realizing I would sound crazy.

"What if we have the cause of death wrong?" I asked quietly.

Jeremy snorted derisively. "What are you saying, Jacks? He was—"

"What if the shotgun blast isn't what killed him?"

Chapter Fifteen

Opening Head Rock Harbor Books first thing Friday morning was non-negotiable. After being closed all day Thursday without explanation, I had regular customers who were foaming at the mouth and revving up the rumor mill. When you find a dead body on a Sunday, make a scene at your mother's restaurant, have been seen storming in and out of the police department, and then close your shop without explanation on a random Thursday, people talk. Obviously, I'd been arrested for the murder of Carter Nelson, or had, in some way, been implicated in his death. That's why Head Rock Harbor Books didn't open on Thursday.

The Head Rock Harbor Prayer Chain was quite active, but rarely correct.

Fortunately, by mid-morning, word was beginning to spread that the bookstore was open again, and I'd been cleared of all—*imaginary*—charges. It only took a handful of customers in the morning hours to see me behind the check-out counter before the rumors were put to rest. Regardless of my exoneration in the shortest trial of public opinion ever, I was still bothered. Anyone thinking I had something to do with someone's death—or feeling I could even be implicated in such a thing—hurt a bit.

All of us can keep stiff upper lips and stand with our backs straight and our shoulders set all we want, but having your fellow townsfolk believing you capable of great violence stings. Even the toughest among us would feel a bit hurt by such a thing. And I was no different. Though I was perfectly pleasant and helpful as I always was with my customers, I was unhappy throughout most of the morning.

Rattlesnatches, sensing my disappointment with my fellow humans, refused to come down from his perches to be petted or fawned over. He stayed atop the bookshelves, glaring down at all who dared pass by. Imparting heinous judgment upon the citizens of Head Rock Harbor who had thought poorly of me—if only for a day—was his gift to me. I greatly appreciated it. Especially since I knew how much he loved to have customers fawn over him.

By the time lunch came around, I was considering making Friday a half day. However, I knew that after shutting down one rumor, changing operating hours randomly would only make the next rumor worse. Realizing that there was nothing to be done about how smalltown gossip works, I decided that the new operating hours of Head Rock Harbor Books would start immediately.

Busying myself over the next half hour, I made a reasonably professional looking, handwritten sign for the front door of the shop. It would have to be enough to inform my customers of the new hours. After a few days my clientele would adjust to the new hours. There might be a few complaints during that period, but it would end quickly.

Upon examining my handiwork and giving the sign an affirmative and pleased nod of my head, I decided to close up for lunch. After turning off the lights and grabbing my wallet and keys, I grabbed a book I'd set aside on the check-out counter. Titled "Post Mortem," it was a guide to all things about the human body—and what happens to it—after death.

With the book tucked under my arm, I made my way down Harbor Street for my typical lunch at Munchies. The breeze coming off the river was crisp and still carried a hint of winter, so without a jacket, I rushed down the street. Rushing into Munchies to escape the cold, my head was down as I held the book to my side. When I ran into what felt like a padded wall right inside the front door, I nearly dropped my book as I stepped back.

"*Well, Jackson!*" A voice rang out as I collected myself and corrected my stance.

Looking around for what I'd run into, my eyes landed on Myrna Nelson. Straightening herself, a to-go bag held at her side, she looked ruffled, but amused. Immediately I was embarrassed at having plowed directly into her. Of course, unintentionally running down one of Munchies' customers concerned me. Would I be banned from my favorite lunch spot if I couldn't be trusted to watch my step? I tried not to chuckle at the thought as I straightened myself.

"Myrna!" I said. "I'm so sorry. I was trying to get out of the cold and—"

"Oh," she said, waving me off, "don't worry about it. You're fine. No harm done."

Shirley was shaking her head and chuckling at the check-out counter as the two of us said our apologies. Myrna, for what it was worth, seemed mostly unfazed by having me run her down as she tried to exit the café. I, on the other hand, felt as though I'd slapped her across the face. Typically, I have spatial awareness and manners. The cold breeze had made me lose both long enough to assault another human being, no matter how unintentional.

"If it's the worst thing that happens to me today, it'll be a good day," Myrna chuckled.

"I guess that's fair," I said. "Sorry again."

"My food is okay, so I'll let you have a pass this time," she said with a wink, then held up her to-go bag to jiggle it at me.

Laughing, I took notice of the bag that held her to-go order. Large enough for a decent lunch, but too small to feed more than one person, I realized Myrna wasn't intending to feed a crowd.

"You're not feeding your boys?" I asked.

Myrna looked at her bag.

"Just me," she said, lowering the bag to her side. "All of the boys are off comforting Colton."

She shook her head ruefully.

"I don't think that boy will ever get over his daddy doing what he did," Myrna sighed.

"I can imagine," I replied.

Standing there looking at Myrna, shaking her head as she looked down at her feet, I couldn't help but feel sorry for the Nelsons. Even if there was something wrong about Carter's death, real people were impacted by his passing, regardless of the cause. It was obvious, standing there in Munchies, that his sister missed him terribly. Having to help his bereaved son get over his grief while she was dealing with her own had to be awful.

I couldn't help but wonder if Jeremy and I poking around in the peculiarity of Carter's death wasn't going to cause more harm than good. If after all of our detective work, we found out that the irregularities between the crime scene and the medical examiner's report was nothing, I'd feel awful. We would be creating more trauma for the Nelson family than was necessary. Was the information and evidence I'd found really enough to risk such thing?

Myrna's face, when she looked up, made me wonder.

"My boys would do anything for their cousin," she said. "Anything."

I nodded slowly.

"They're taking this almost as hard as he is," she added.

"I'm sure it's difficult for everyone." I reached out and squeezed her upper arm.

Myrna did her best to give me a smile, so I gave her arm another squeeze before dropping my hand back to my side.

"I'm just glad my boys are here to make sure Colton is protected," Myrna said. "It's what Carter would have wanted. No matter what."

I didn't tell Myrna that I didn't know Carter so I couldn't explicitly agree. However, though it had not been my own personal experience, I assumed most fathers cared for their sons that much. Myrna gave me another smile, which I returned.

"Well," she said, "I better get home and tear into this before it gets cold. Enjoy your lunch, Jackson."

She jiggled her bag at me again and stepped around me to the door.

"You too," I said quietly as Myrna exited Munchies.

I watched through the front window as Myrna opened the passenger door of her car parked out on the curb outside Munchies. She set the bag carefully in the seat and closed the door. Dashing around the front of the car, she opened the driver's door and slid in behind the wheel. A moment after fastening her seatbelt, she took off slowly down Harbor Street.

I felt like crap.

"You gonna have a seat?" Shirley's voice woke me from my daydream.

I looked over at her at the counter and smiled wanly.

"I'll be over there," I said, crooking my head at the booth in the front window.

"You want your usual, hon?" she asked.

"Yeah," I said, "the usual. Thanks, Shirley."

Chapter Sixteen

The rest of my Friday at the bookstore was uneventful. Plenty of books moved from the shelves—the weekend readers were getting stocked up for their days off. When I wasn't selling books, I was explaining, as patiently as possible, to my regulars about the new hours for Head Rock Harbor Books. By the end of the work day, I had at least a dozen different ways to explain that the bookstore hours would be changing.

I'd intended to cook dinner instead of going out for the second time in a day, but the draw of not doing dishes found me walking to Harper's once I closed up shop. Rattlesnatches was unhappy seeing me leave him alone once again, but it was a cross he was going to have to bear. Instead of bothering with the Beetle, I decided to walk over to Harper's. Since I had promised Jeremy I'd sneak over to his place after dark to look at the medical examiner's report, walking was best. Being discrete was pointless if my car was seen sitting outside his house, after all.

A typical Friday night was underway when I finally found myself walking up to the front door of my mother's bar and grill. Rowdy townsfolk who had shown up for drinking, dancing, and pool playing could be heard before I even opened the front door. Fortunately, upon entering Harper's, I found that the rowdiness in the bar area meant that the restaurant area was only half full. I had my choice of seats.

Heidi, the hostess, waved me towards the dining area and I gave her a polite nod. A minute later and I was sliding into my favorite corner booth. It was a good spot to watch the entire room, feel like I was part of the crowd, but removed from the craziness. And Harper's could absolutely be crazy on a Friday evening. It wasn't the type of chaos I liked to be a part of, either.

Due to the crowd in the bar area and the half full dining area, it took a while before Deb showed up at my table to take my order. Typically, having time to go over the menu is a good thing. However, when you're eating at your mother's restaurant, have the menu memorized, and also order the same thing every time, it was pointless for me. Waiting to order was an inconvenience more than anything.

"Same as usual?" Deb asked quickly.

"Not even a 'hi, son' or anything?" I teased.

Deb huffed. "We're busy. Or could you not tell?"

She jutted her head towards the bar area and jabbed her hands into her hips. Sass, thy name is Deborah Harper.

"Jeez," I said, "I was just trying to lighten the mood."

Her expression softened but her hands didn't leave her hips.

"When you come over there and help mix and pour drinks for these fools, the mood will lighten," she said. "Now, if it's the usual, just say so."

"The usual," I said.

"Good." Deb nodded and marched away.

Rolling my eyes, I settled into my booth and pulled out my phone. I scanned through my social media apps, which were pathetically dry. I'd never been one for putting my life all over the internet, using the apps solely to keep in touch with friends and family. Considering that I still lived in my hometown and most of my college friends lived busy lives, there wasn't much to see in my mentions.

Logging into the Instagram account I had for Head Rock Harbor Books was an entirely different monster. *The Quaint Bookstore on the River*—as it had been dubbed by numerous publications in the state, the bookstore had ten times as many followers as its owner. Jackson Harper wasn't all that popular, but the books he sold were A-list celebrities. Rattlesnatches had a bit of a following himself. All of the bookstore posts that included him always racked up hundreds of likes within a day.

For a bookstore in a tiny tourist town in east central Iowa, Head Rock Harbor Books didn't do too bad. If it weren't for the royalties from my book sales, it would make me a meager living. However, for a bookstore in the twenty-first century, a "meager living" was sometimes the best one could hope for in such an enterprise.

I found myself wondering if things wouldn't be better if I didn't clear a corner of the store for a coffee bar. Hire a barista. Serve simple coffee drinks. Head Rock Harbor didn't really have a coffee shop. Unless you counted the

Starbucks out on the highway by the hospital. I, for one, did not count that as coffee.

Making a mental note to post more pictures of books—preferably with Rattlesnatches nearby—on Instagram, I felt my mind wander. I was never one for chasing the next big thing or making my life more complicated. I liked my easy life in the bookstore, selling books, writing my books, being an anonymous bestselling author, and keeping my head low.

Opening a coffee bar and posting more to social media could change things.

I wasn't certain that I wanted things to be different.

Becoming so engrossed with my phone, I barely noticed the restaurant slowly emptying out as I waited for my dinner. When I looked up from playing a round of a silly word game on my phone, I realized that only two other tables held diners. With a furrowed brow, I leaned over to look around the restaurant for Deb. It wasn't like Beau to take too long to get orders out of the kitchen, and it wasn't like Deb to forget me, either.

I was about to slide out of my booth and find my mother to see if she'd forgotten to put my order in when Cleo pushed through the swinging kitchen door. Her apologetic gaze landed on me as she jiggled the plate in her hand at me. I settled back into the booth, giving her a smile. Obviously, things had gotten incredibly busy if Cleo was bringing my order out.

Cleo St. Clair was the bartender for Harper's Bar, Grill, Bait & Tackle. She worked all six days the joint was open and rarely, if ever, did any duties outside of the bar area. However, when the kitchen was really in the weeds, she'd chip in from time to time. Usually, between Deb and Heidi, the restaurant ran smoothly. Some days didn't go according to plan, though.

"Sorry, Jackson," Cleo said as she stopped next to my table. "Things are crazy over at the bar."

"Then why are you here?" I chuckled as she set my plate on the table.

Cleo laughed with me.

"Your mom said I could *finally* have a break if I would bring your food to you first," she replied. "Seemed like a decent deal to me."

I looked down at my Philly cheesesteak, rings, and coleslaw.

"Don't worry," Cleo said. "It's all fresh and warm. Beau got a little behind. That's what took so long. That and all the fools over there."

She waved an exhausted arm towards the other side of the building. Following her gesture, my eyes drifted over to the bar. The crowd definitely seemed rowdier than usual. Folks were dancing excitedly near the jukebox, a group was crowded around the pool table, and the bar was two people deep, looking for rounds of drinks. The craziness of the bar was what drew my attention to a specific person immediately.

In the far corner of the bar area, sat alone, was Colton Nelson. Amongst the throng of revelers, he stood out, simply because he was by far the least rowdy of all. Once again, I'd found him drinking alone in Harper's. I frowned to myself as I watched him for a moment. It took Cleo speaking up to draw my attention back to the here and now.

"Everything okay?" she asked.

"Oh," I said, looking at my plate as if I'd never seen it before, "yeah. It looks great."

"Good. I'll check back in on you when I'm done with my break," Cleo said.

Before she could walk away, I spoke up.

"Hey," I said, "can I ask you a question? Maybe three."

Cleo stood next to the table and crossed her arms over her chest and stared down at me.

"When my break runs over, you're going to explain it to your mother," she said.

"Fair enough," I said with a laugh. "I'll make it quick."

Cleo shrugged and slid into the booth across from me. She groaned at the relief of finally being off of her feet for once in the evening. Even though Cleo wore combat boots—typically easier on the feet than many women's shoes—a night on your feet was still rough.

"And I'd appreciate it if you didn't tell Deb I asked you about this," I said quietly.

Cleo leaned in, lacing her fingers on top of the table.

"Oooooh," she cooed, "I'm intrigued."

Chuckling, I asked, "Does Colton Nelson come in here every night to drink? You know, since his dad...died?"

With a softening of her face, Cleo nodded.

"Seen him every night since," she said, reaching up to brush her black bangs out of her face. "Drinks himself stupid every night."

"His cousins never come with him?"

"They're here tonight." Cleo frowned. "But they kind of...let him wallow? I guess? They make sure he gets home safely every night. We make sure."

I nodded.

"It's just rough losing a parent that way," Cleo said. "So, we don't treat him like the other drunks around here. He doesn't cause trouble. We leave him be and let his cousins deal with the rest."

"Seems fair," I said.

Cleo waited as I picked up an onion ring and popped it in my mouth. Chewing deliberately, I tried to figure out how to ask my next question without being too obvious.

"So," I asked, "they were all here together the night Carter died? They never left?"

Cleo grinned impishly.

"Very slick," she said. "Yes. They were all here together that night."

"Sorry," I said. "I didn't mean to insult your intelligence."

"You wouldn't be the first man tonight to do so." Cleo shrugged. "But your reasons are better than most."

We both laughed.

"They never left or anything?" I asked. "They all just drank here until closing?"

Cleo nodded a few times, then stopped. Suddenly, she looked thoughtful.

"What is it?" I asked.

She considered me for a moment before speaking.

"Well," Cleo began, "this is ridiculous. And I'm not playing into your little Detective Jackson thing you've got going on here—"

"Of course, not."

"—but, I mean, they all left at one point or another. For a little bit. But just to step outside. And never together."

That gave me something to think about.

"How long did they leave for?"

Cleo shrugged. "A few minutes each. I think they were stepping out to…"

She made a smoking gesture that indicated they partook in something besides cigarettes. I grinned and nodded. Cleo looked thoughtful.

"But not Colton. Other than going to the bathroom, he was in here all night. It was just the other three. They were all here to show Colton a good time though, I think, so it was only one of them gone at a time. They didn't leave him alone or anything."

"It'd be rude to take him out and ditch him for…*a smoke*," I said.

Cleo gave me a smile and gestured vaguely.

"Any other questions?"

"I've taken up enough of your time," I said, waving her off. "Go take your break and tell Deb it's all my fault you needed a few extra minutes. She can be mad at me."

Cleo reached across the table to pat my forearm before sliding out of the booth and making her way back to the kitchen. I was lifting my sandwich to my mouth by the time the kitchen door was swinging once again.

I made quick work of my sandwich and rings, then took out the bowl of coleslaw. Knowing that my tab was covered by my mother's generosity, I left a cash tip on the table and exited the booth. With a full belly, I made my way to the front door. As I headed through the restaurant, my eyes were drawn to the bar, and once again, Colton caught my attention.

Seeing him so lonely—and drunk—amongst all of the rowdiness had me changing course. Instead of heading to the front door, I found my feet carrying me towards the bar.

Before I could cross over from the restaurant into the bar, I found my path blocked by none other than Kenny Nelson. Looking up at him, I did my best to smile.

"Hey, Kenny," I said.

He had inserted himself in front of me in a way that blocked my forward momentum, but wasn't necessarily imposing. Kenny leaned a shoulder against the frame of the large doorway into the bar.

"Jackson," he nodded. "What's going on with you?"

"Just had dinner," I jerked my head towards the back booth.

He nodded slowly. "Look, if you're thinking about talking to Colton, could you not?"

"I'm sorry?" My brow raised.

Kenny looked around furtively. "He told me you talked to him the other night. You've talked to mom. We saw you at Munchies. I just think it's best if you stop bringing up Carter's death. It's making things worse for Colton."

I glanced past Kenny to find Colton still sitting at his table in the bar, alone, drinking, unaware of everything going on around him.

"I'd really appreciate it," Kenny said firmly.

I looked up at him, then my eyes shot over to the bar. Deb was behind the bar, pouring a beer from the tap, but her eyes were locked firmly on Kenny and me. Kenny, following my eyes, took notice of Deb. He pushed away from the doorframe.

"It'd be best," he said with finality.

Then he turned and walked away to the pool table to join his brothers. I looked over at Deb and she gave me the "whose butt do I need to kick" look she'd been giving me since I was a child. Smiling softly, I shook my head at her and she nodded back, then returned to making drinks. Frowning at the Carter boys over at the pool table, shooting glances in my direction as they whispered, I turned on my heels and left Harper's.

Chapter Seventeen

"So, I've been trying to wrap my mind around this," Jeremy said, leaning against the kitchen bar.

I was seated on one of the stools on the other side of the bar, poring over the contents of the medical examiner's report as he spoke. Having been reading the report in silence for several minutes, Jeremy's statement shook me from my spell. He was scratching his fingers through his messy golden curls, his eyes squinted in thought, as the corner of his mouth turned up in frustration.

After leaving Harper's, I'd booked it over to Jeremy's, making it in record time. For some reason, my encounter with Kenny Nelson had me spooked. All the way to Jeremy's little ranch-style house, I'd been glancing over my shoulder. I had no reason to think I was in danger, but Kenny had given me concern. I couldn't quite place my finger on what he'd said that had unnerved me so, but that concern sat in my belly like lead.

Ultimately, being a gay guy living in middle America, I was always conscious of the dangers the world posed. When

I had a terse encounter with someone, that only heightened the alertness. Kenny Nelson hadn't said anything to indicate that I needed to watch my back, but I wasn't stupid. I knew a warning when I heard it, regardless of the words used.

"Wrap your mind around what?" I asked.

"*What if the shotgun blast isn't what killed him*?" Jeremy said. "I've been thinking about it since you left last night. I heard it in my dreams."

Laughing gently, I glanced down at the report and decided to ignore it for a moment.

"Sorry I invaded your dreams."

Jeremy chuckled nervously.

"What is it about it that's bothering you?" I asked. "I mean, it was just a thought. I don't really have a theory as to—"

"Why would he shoot himself then?" Jeremy interrupted me. "What was the point? I mean, if he knew he was dying? Why then shoot yourself?"

Thinking about that, I shrugged.

"Maybe he didn't pull the trigger?" I suggested.

"So, someone else put him out of his misery like a horse?" Jeremy laughed.

It was morbid, but I couldn't help but laugh with him.

"It still doesn't explain the livor mortis, the body positioning…I think you said that just to get under my skin, Jacks," Jeremy said with a grin.

"No," I replied. "I really didn't. It was a theory. Nothing else. I wasn't trying to mess with you."

Jeremy eyed me.

"Promise."

"Okay," he said, waving me off. "So, I think I'm dropping that theory. I'm forgetting you said it. Hopefully, it'll stay out of my dreams tonight."

"Fair enough."

I turned my attention back to the report. As I'd seen for myself in the morgue with Deacon, the livor mortis was noted in the report. Bruising on the side of Carter Nelson's head was mentioned. Abrasions on his chin and chest. The gunshot wound was described in copious detail that was difficult to read, especially on a full stomach. His bisected aorta was mentioned again. He had superficial scrapes all over his body.

That made my brow furrow.

Apparently, according to the report, the shotgun was filled with birdshot. At close range, for example, with the muzzle of the shotgun to his chest, birdshot did a perfect job of stirring up Carter's insides. I grimaced as I thought of the wound. I'd done my best over the week to forget Carter's death scene, but it was impossible. Anytime I thought of it, that gaping wound in his chest flashed through my mind.

Fortunately, I didn't have the problem of bad dreams like Jeremy. Revisiting that scene nightly when I was powerless would have been torture.

"Well," I pushed the report back to Jeremy, "I guess I've read it."

Jeremy took the report and folded it shut.

"And?" he asked.

I shrugged. Jeremy chuckled at me.

"I was at Harper's before I came here," I said. "Had dinner. It was busy."

"Yeah?"

"Kenny Nelson kind of...I don't know...tried to intimidate me."

Jeremy tensed. "What?"

"He blocked me from talking to Colton," I explained. "Kind of bowed up at me. Essentially told me to stop digging into Carter's death."

Jeremy straightened. "I'll go kick his—"

"Stop." I waved him off with a laugh. "I can handle Kenny Nelson. I think."

"He's not going to tell you what to do," Jeremy barked.

"My hero," I said, holding my hand to my chest. "Seriously, let it go. I was just telling you since it might be important in some way."

Jeremy rolled his eyes, but relaxed a little.

"You sure?" he asked. "I can have him in a jail cell in ten minutes."

"That would be an abuse of your badge, Germ," I said. "He didn't do anything illegal."

"Threatening you was—"

"He didn't *threaten* me. It was...circumspect."

He frowned.

"But it was weird," I said with a shrug. "I got the message without him using his big boy words."

Sitting there at the kitchen bar with Jeremy standing opposite me, I knew that I'd discovered nothing new from the medical examiner's report. I'd begged for it for nothing. There was nothing in the report of consequence that gave me greater insight into Carter Nelson's death. The official cause of death had been ruled the shotgun blast to his chest.

Apparent suicide.

I still couldn't wrap my head around that decision. Who in their right mind committed suicide with a shotgun in the way that Carter Nelson presumably had? It was completely atypical and nearly physically impossible. Not to say that Carter couldn't have pulled it off—desperate people manage incredible feats all of the time. It was simply highly unlikely that a person could hold a shotgun to their chest, reach to pull the trigger, shoot themselves, and then fall forward.

Especially while lying on the ground.

"Jeremy," I said, "if you held a shotgun to your chest and pulled the trigger to kill yourself, how accurate could you be?"

"Huh?" I looked over to see him staring at me.

"Wouldn't the shotgun kick back? Wouldn't a person more than likely end up shooting themselves higher in the chest? The neck? Even part of their face? A shotgun has a pretty good kick, right?"

He thought about that.

"Well, yeah," he said finally. "The fact that the wound was relatively clean and centralized, that is odd. You'd think there'd be more than one big hole."

I grimaced, but kept my dinner down.

"The report," I tapped the file with an index finger, "indicates that the centralized pellet pattern, the exorbitant amount of gunpowder residue on the clothing and skin, and the burn marks on the clothing suggests the shotgun was held right against Carter's chest. Hard to do to yourself."

Even considering our best theory, I couldn't get my head to process what I'd seen, what I'd heard, and what I'd read. Everything—all of the information I had—was like a tornado in my head. Whipping and whirling around, refusing to settle so that the debris could be examined and put back together. Carter Nelson's death was suspicious. But no solid theory as to why would form in my head.

"I'm going to go home," I said, standing from the stool.

Jeremy sighed.

"Let me drive you," he said as I made my way to the end of the bar.

"No," I replied. "Don't put yourself out. You just got home after a long day."

"After the thing with Kenny at Harper's, I want to make sure you get home safe," Jeremy said, coming to meet me at the end of the bar.

I said, "It really wasn't a threat, it was just—"

"Let me have my keys, Jacks!" Jeremy grinned and darted an arm around me.

I feinted to the side to block him.

As Jeremy reached around me to grab his keys from the bar, we were suddenly so close that I could feel his body heat. I froze and Jeremy mimicked me, stuck in place with his face next to mine. I heard his keys jingle on the counter, so his fingers were the only part of him moving. He turned his head to look into my eyes and I found I was holding my breath.

For several moments, we stared into each other's eyes, the silence of his kitchen so profound I felt as if I was wearing earmuffs. My heart was thudding in my chest, but I found that I couldn't breathe. Jeremy's Adam's apple bobbed in his throat as he looked into my eyes. He gave no indication that he was going to move away.

Finally, I found my breath, and with a quick inhale, I ducked around him, putting space between us. His keys jingled on the counter again, and when I turned to look at him, with more space between us, he had turned to look at me.

"I can make my own way home," I said softly.

"I'd feel better if I could take you," he replied as quietly. "Please?"

I nodded. "Okay."

It was a quiet ride back to the bookstore, but fortunately, it was brief. It wasn't until I was inside of the store with the door locked behind that I could breathe correctly. I watched from the window of the unlit store as Jeremy drove slowly away down Harbor Street.

Chapter Eighteen

"You know what you need?"

I'd been working on the latest *Detective Randy Melton Mystery series* book at the check-out counter when a voice disturbed me. Saturday morning at the bookstore had been slow to start, so I'd seen no reason to not multi-task. Make book. Sell books. It was logical to me. However, writing downstairs in the shop during business hours brought the risk of being interrupted.

Interruptions for a writer—or any creative—are the killer of the muse. As soon as the flow began and the words flew from my fingertips, inevitably, someone would need something. And unlike other situations where being interrupted while working was simply annoying, being interrupted while writing my books was dangerous.

No one besides my agent, editor, and publisher knew that I was behind the best-selling *Detective Randy Melton Mystery series*. I wanted to keep it that way. So, writing in the shop brought the risk of being exposed. When someone approached the check-out counter, or interrupted me in some other way, I had to close my laptop. Otherwise, there was the danger of them getting a look at the screen.

Head Rock Harbor, aside from two murders and a questionable suicide, was a fairly crime-free town. Sure, we had barroom brawls, parking and speeding tickets, and a few incidents of public intoxication. Theft and robbery were uncommon. However, bringing my laptop downstairs did run the risk of those with sticky fingers helping them to my property. A laptop is easy to snatch and take off with if a thief felt the urge.

Fortunately, writing at the check-out counter hadn't produced any real problems. Inconveniences and annoyances, yes. That's simply a writer's cross to bear, though.

Looking up, I found Sawyer Robison standing on the other side of the counter, a grin on his face and a stack of books cradled to his chest.

"Hand carts?" I eyed the stack of books.

Chuckling, he said, "A coffee bar. Maybe a few chairs."

"Why?"

Asking for a reason was pointless since I'd been considering the option for a while myself. However, I wanted a loyal customer's opinion on the matter.

"I've been in here an hour," Sawyer said. "I don't think you've even noticed me."

"Sorry," I cringed.

"It's okay," Sawyer said, setting the stack of books on the counter. "You seem busy. And I know how to find what I want."

"Apparently."

"But if you had a coffee bar, I could order a coffee, leisurely browse, and even have a place to sit and read and sip my coffee when I'm done."

Nodding, I began to ring up his purchases. Sawyer came into Head Rock Harbor Books often—he was my biggest sci-fi fan—but sometimes he showed up and bought a stockpile of books. This usually indicated that he was going to have time off to partake in his favorite hobby—doing nothing with a book.

"I've thought about it," I said. "But it'll take some time. Did you see the new hours?"

He nodded. "You deserve two days off in a row."

"Thank you," I paused the checking out process to look at him. "Thank you very much. You're the first customer to understand and not complain."

We both laughed, fully aware of the attitudes of the citizens of Head Rock Harbor.

Sawyer set about extracting his wallet from his back pocket while I finished ringing up his books. As prolific a reader as Sawyer was, I was surprised that he'd found any books in the Sci-Fi section he hadn't read. In fact, as much as he read, I was always nearly compelled to suggest he get a library card. However, losing sales from Sawyer would put a dent in my business, so I decided it wasn't entirely unethical to keep my mouth shut.

Maybe he was a collector. It wasn't my business. Selling books was.

"So," Sawyer moved up, leaning into the counter casually, "they still bothering you about the whole…*Carter thing*?"

The corner of my mouth quirked with frustration.

"They're always bothering me," I said. "But no. I'm pretty sure I was cleared as soon as they got the GSR test back."

Sawyer snorted.

"Same," he said. "Which surprises me."

We both exchanged a look of understanding. Things such as they were in smalltown America, Sawyer's skin tone could have easily kept him on the PD's radar longer. Fortunately, though it wasn't completely free of bias and prejudice, Head Rock Harbor wasn't outwardly racist. And Marv, Jeremy, and Riley were unlikely to base their evidence around a person's blackness. They had their own issues, but racists they were not.

"Anyway, I'm just glad to be cleared," he said with finality. "Especially since there's obviously a murderer loose."

My head shot up to look at him as he handed me his debit card.

"Why do you say that?" I asked quickly.

Sawyer snorted derisively again.

"Between you and me, Jackson, that scene was suspicious. And I know if I noticed it, *you* noticed it. Don't act like you didn't."

I ran Sawyer's payment as I thought about how I wanted to respond.

"I know you don't want to talk bad about your boy Jeremy, but—"

"He's not my boy," I said quickly, handing him his card. "Jeremy. We're not *boys*. He's my friend. That's all."

A slow smile overtook Sawyer's face as he slid his wallet into his back pocket without breaking eye contact.

"Well, I know you don't want to think he's a bad cop. But if he can't see that something was wrong out in those woods, then he's a bad cop."

I didn't have anything to say to that. Saying that Jeremy was still investigating could get word back to Marv that he was being disobeyed. Pretending Jeremy wasn't investigating proved Sawyer's theory. I smiled and handed Sawyer his bag.

"Enjoy your books," I said simply. "See you next week for your next big haul."

He laughed and headed to the door, the bag dangling from his fingertips. When he reached the door, he swung the bag over his shoulder, which produced a loud "thump" against his muscular back. Sawyer turned, his hand on the doorknob, and met my eyes.

"Good to know," he said.

"What's good to know?" I asked.

"Jeremy," he said. "That he's not your *boy*."

I shrugged.

"We should get back out on the river sometime," Sawyer said vaguely. "When you have a minute."

Wondering how I'd gone from having the driest romantic life in the world to two guys asking me out in a week made my head spin.

"I'm off Sundays and Mondays," I said. "As you now know."

I waved a hand at the sign on the door.

Sawyer gave me an upward nod.

"Keep next Sunday open," he said. "I like getting the boat out on Sundays. As you know."

"All right," I said slowly. "Hopefully we won't find a body next time."

Sawyer laughed and exited the store with a hollered promise over his shoulder to text me later. Sitting there and thinking about the exchange I'd had with an incredibly attractive man was appealing, but my mind was elsewhere. Sawyer's comment about the scene in the woods had gotten the brain matter twitching. Instead of sitting around in a quiet shop, working on my book, I locked my laptop and stored it under the counter.

Grabbing my jacket, keys, wallet, and phone, I hurried out of the shop. Rattlesnatches gave me a disdainful look from his perch in the window as I left, but I ignored him. I'd give him a larger dinner portion for putting up with all of my absences. In the meantime, he'd have to suck it up and suffer without me.

A quick ten-minute walk later, and I was crossing Wilford Street via the trail into the woods. As I was sliding down the pathway into the woods, I regretted not changing my shoes before leaving the bookstore. My work loafers were no match for the soft forest ground typical of Spring. Knowing that I would have to practically hose my shoes off when I got home had me cringing as I concentrated on not falling.

It took some doing, between my shoes and the soggy ground, but I finally found my way out to the area that had been Carter's and Colton's campsite. Frowning, I noticed that the police department had already cleared any evidence of its existence. Every last piece of the campsite was gone. If I hadn't seen the site for myself, seen where Carter had died, I would have been convinced that I was in the wrong spot.

As I stood in the small clearing between the trees, I sighed, wondering what it was that I actually thought I was going to find. Jeremy and Marv had seen to having the scene thoroughly combed for evidence. Even if there had been something to find, it had been taken away by Deacon and anyone else working forensics. The mud clumped up on the sides and bottoms of my shoes had been for naught. Carter Nelson was dead, and the reason why was not going to be found at the former campsite.

Not anymore.

There were no more missing buttons. I wasn't going to find a missed shotgun shell. A shoeprint that didn't belong to Carter wasn't going to produce a new theory—besides, too many people, including me, had walked through the campsite since his death. If someone else was responsible for his death, they weren't going to leap out from behind a tree and expose themselves.

This wasn't a detective novel where the villain was going to show up for the third act and explain why, how, when, and where. Expecting the murderer—if there even was one—to show up and reveal the details of their nefarious plot was ridiculous. Ideal...but ridiculous. Besides, villains with a third act reveal usually have the detective at their mercy first, and I wanted to avoid that situation. Being tied to a creaky wooden chair did nothing for my back.

With an exasperated huff, I whipped around, planning to head back to the trail. As I turned, the mud on my shoes, still slick with wet, made me lose my balance. Before I could reach out for something, anything to stop my descent, I was falling to the ground. A second after I fell, a shot rang out.

My backside connected with the ground as the bark of the tree behind me splintered.

For a moment, I thought that I'd imagined the sound of the gunshot. The hurt radiating up my spine had my head foggy. My vision blurred for the briefest of moments as I let out a gust of breath and a groan. Confusion settled in momentarily as I pushed my hands into the soft earth, trying to lift myself.

My head was just beginning to clear and the ringing in my ears was lessening as another shot rang out. As the wood in the trunk of the tree behind me took another splintering, my head jerked up in alarm. A life-threatening second passed as I processed what was going on, but then I pushed myself from the ground violently.

Before I knew what was going on, I was dashing away from the campsite, slipping and sliding in the muck in my loafers. When I finally got into the cover of the trees, I kicked off my shoes as I ran, leaving them in the mud behind me. Trees whipped by, their spindly limbs whipping at my cheeks as I ran away from a danger I couldn't see.

Wincing at the pain from the woods grabbing and slapping at me, I continued to run. The rocks and undergrowth tore at my feet through my socks as I continued to run. Heaving breaths made my lungs burn in the early Spring air as I put space between myself and the campsite.

Two more gunshots went off behind me. I had no idea if the trees around me were taking damage like the one at the campsite, but I didn't stop to find out. When a third shot rang out, panic set in, even though I seemed to be getting away from whomever was shooting at me. I've never been much of a runner, so I wasn't sure if my gasping breaths were from exertion or fear, but I felt fear had the majority stake.

Running back up the hill at the edge of the woods was nearly impossible, but somehow, I managed. If I'd still had my loafers on, I wouldn't have been able to do it. By the time I burst out of the woods and was sliding across the pavement of Wilford Street in my mud-caked socks, I could barely breathe. The shots behind me had stopped, but I refused to let my burning chest force me to stop running.

I did the only thing I could think of that would protect me from anyone chasing me with a gun. My eyes landed on the trailer park, and I changed direction, dashing for the one place I knew I would be safe. Even if the person who had shot at me in the woods followed, they'd be sorry they hadn't given up chase.

By the time I had dashed up the steps of Mavis' trailer and onto her covered deck, leaving muddy footprints behind, my socks were shredded. From the pain in my soles, I knew my feet had to be scratched, cut up, and bleeding. Ignoring the pain in my feet and the intense burning in my chest, I banged on her trailer door.

"*Mavis!*" I hollered.

The string of multi-colored party lights that hung over her door rattled against the metal trailer as my fist assaulted her home.

"*Let me in, Mavis!*" I huffed, out of breath. "*Please!*"

After a few seconds of knocking and no answer, I reached down and ripped my socks off in a panic, tossing them off the deck. I reached for the knob, found it unlocked, and let myself into the house. Quickly, I stumbled into the house, gasping for breath, but relieved at the feeling of carpet against my feet. The fact that I could be bleeding on Mavis' carpet was of no concern at the moment.

I'll buy you new carpet. I thought to myself.

Twisting my head back and forth, I found the trailer dark. Sunlight did it's best to slither through the heavy curtains of the trailer's windows, but gloom pervaded. Slapping at the wall, I finally found the light switch. The overhead fan and light came on with a soft "whir" sound and I blinked my eyes.

Mavis was nowhere to be found.

"*Mavis!*" I hollered again.

Nothing. I looked down the hall that led to the bathroom and bedroom, but darkness pervaded in that area of the trailer.

"Mavis?" I asked in a questioning tone as the burning in my chest lessened.

I concentrated on slowing my breathing, on chasing away the panic in my chest. It took a moment, but I finally could breathe somewhat normally. Once I had most of my wits about me, I spun back to the front door to where Mavis kept her shotgun. Even if she wasn't home, I knew enough to operate a shotgun.

Point and pull the trigger.

If the person who had tried to shoot me had followed me to Mavis' trailer, they'd be sorry if they came through her front door.

When I found the spot where the shotgun always leaned empty, I frowned. Mavis always left her shotgun by the front door. In case someone tried to break in—or a Girl Scout wouldn't take "no" for an answer.

I spun around, looking for where Mavis had put her shotgun. She'd likely laid it down somewhere without thinking. The battered wooden coffee table held a half-empty coffee mug and a full ashtray. The sofa and easy chair with brown and orange floral patterns meant for three decades ago were empty and threadbare as usual. The yellowed Formica countertops of the kitchen held nothing, save a few crumbs left from her last meal.

Panic began to set in again as I realized that I was safer than I'd been in the open, but I was still without much of a defense. If the person who had tried to shoot me had seen where I'd gone, it wouldn't be long before they burst through the door. Having the door swing open and finding a shotgun leveling at me, looking into the eyes of my killer a second before death came, would severely ruin my day.

As the thought entered my head, the door actually did swing open. I ducked out of instinct, crouching until my knees popped. When Mavis stepped into the house, cursing and stomping her feet, I sighed with relief. She'd cursed and stomped a few times, shut the door behind her, and taken her coat off before she even noticed me. When she turned to see me rising from my crouch, she let out an expletive-laden gasp. Out of instinct, she turned quickly to grab her shotgun.

Finding the spot empty as she realized who was actually in her house, she paused. With a confused look on her face, she turned to me. A frown prickled at the corners of her mouth, though I wasn't sure why.

"Mavis," I said, smiling at my fortune. "Sorry, Mavis. I needed somewhere to go and I was in the woods and—"

"What are you doin', Jackson?" she asked, her hands going to her hips.

"—I didn't meant to just let myself in, but I was in the woods and—"

Mavis' eyes darted from me to the spot by the door where her shotgun should have been. I immediately lost the ability to talk, my sentence stopping before I could get another word out. We both stood there in the musty air and silence, her frowning at the spot by the front door and me staring at her.

"Well," Mavis said, finally turning to look at me fully, "you're always welcome here. But you scared the life out of me."

Her eyes darted back to the door.

Swallowing hard, the hairs on my neck rose.

"Whatchu doin' here anyway?" she asked. "You get yourself into trouble?"

My eyes darted to the spot by the door. Every alarm in my head was going off.

Getoutgetoutgetoutgetoutgetout.

Before she could ask any more questions, or find a way to keep me in her trailer, I dashed to the door. Smiling an uncomfortable smile, I pushed past Mavis.

"Sorry," I said quickly, my feet refusing to stop. "I have to go. If I tracked mud, I'll pay to have it cleaned."

"Well, I—"

Mavis was looking down at the floor as I pushed through the door, dashed across the deck, and ran from her trailer.

I didn't bother picking up my socks from the yard.

Chapter Nineteen

Jeremy was brewing a pot of coffee. I was seated at his kitchen table, holding a blanket tightly around me as I picked at a chip in the corner of the battered wood top with my thumbnail. My brain felt like mush, my feet felt like ground meat, and my knees were screaming at me. A chill, impressive even for early Spring in Iowa, had settled into my bones. Of course, it wasn't the cold of the season, it was the cold of death—or having escaped it.

Both of us were silent as the coffee dripped into the carafe, providing the only ambient noise to the small room of Jeremy's ranch-style home. The coolness of the linoleum soothed the raw bottoms of my feet a bit, though the cold did nothing to calm me. My muddy clothes and the scratches that decorated any exposed skin on my body made me look a fright. Jeremy shot looks of concern my way in between waiting impatiently on his coffee machine.

"If you bought a machine that took pods—"

"No one cares right now, Jacks," Jeremy grumbled.

"—I'm just saying that—"

Jeremy slapped the counter, making the coffee machine jostle. The dripping stopped for a split second, then sputtered back to life.

"Didn't I tell you to be careful?" he barked.

I swallowed hard and shivered. Arguing with Jeremy would have been reasonable. I'd done nothing to provoke someone into shooting at me. I hadn't put myself in danger. Instead, danger had found me. Every ounce of energy I had on any given day had vacated the property, though. There was nothing in me to fight with Jeremy.

I'd been shot at in the woods.

Someone had tried to...*kill me.*

"And now," Jeremy shook his head, calming himself. "You could be dead."

"Could be," I said, nodding.

I continued to pick at the chip in the wooden tabletop with my thumbnail. Jeremy sighed.

"After we get you warmed up," Jeremy said, "and you tell me everything that happened, you're getting in the shower. I've got a spare pair of sweats and a t-shirt you can borrow. We'll doctor your cuts and your feet and—"

"Someone tried to *kill me*, Germ," I said, not looking up.

He stopped.

I had nothing more to say. The implication was apparent. Even if I'd found nothing else out in the woods, someone trying to kill me proved the thing we had wanted to prove.

Carter Nelson's death *was* suspicious. Somone knew I suspected as much. And they'd tried to take care of it. Or, at the very least, scare me away from investigating it further. Of course, that gave me something else to think about that calmed me marginally. Had someone tried to kill me...or *scare me*?

"Or scare me." I added. "Doesn't matter which, I guess. Someone was still shooting at me."

My mind flashed to the shotgun that wasn't at Mavis' door. I shivered again. Nothing in the world would make me mention this fact to Jeremy. Or Marv. I didn't care what that fact meant. Even if it had any meaning, telling the police would only lead to one thing. Mavis would never see the light of day again. I didn't have enough facts or evidence to take the risk.

Jeremy sighed as the coffee finished its brew cycle. He pulled two mugs from the cabinet above the machine and poured us each a full one. Finally, he made his way over to the kitchen table and sat down across from me. He slid my mug to be with care and I accepted it gratefully. I didn't even wait for it to cool. I took a healthy gulp, which regardless of how it felt on my tongue, I didn't regret.

Then I wrapped my frozen fingers around the mug and held it tightly on the tabletop before me.

"Why did you even go out there again?" Jeremy asked gently. "What did you hope that would accomplish, Jacks? We could have gone together if you thought there was something to find. You would have been safe. Well, safer."

"I don't know," I said. "But what else could I do? There has to be something somewhere that will clue us in on what actually happened to Carter. Where better to start than where it began?"

Jeremy thought on this a moment and started to speak. The soles of his shoes squeaked against the linoleum as he sat forward. He didn't manage to get a single word from his mouth before I stopped him.

"It had to be one of the Nelson boys," I said, finally looking up. "One of them followed me out there."

The space between Jeremy's brows crinkled.

"Kenny practically threatened me—in not so many words—last night," I said. "It could have been him."

Jeremy shook his head.

"Don't dismiss me," I grumbled. "Kenny could have—"

"When did you go out to the woods, Jacks?"

"I don't know?" I shook my head to clear it. "I got out there maybe...an hour ago?"

"It wasn't the Nelsons," Jeremy said.

"How do you know that?" I demanded. "You can't just—"

"I had all of them in an interrogation room at the PD up until thirty minutes ago," Jeremy stopped me, trying to be gentle. "I got home five minutes before you stumbled up on the porch, Jacks. It couldn't have been them. I had eyes on them."

I slumped in my seat. But my hands didn't leave the mug. Its heavenly warmth was too much to abandon, no matter how frustrated I had become. If the Nelsons had been at the police department with Jeremy, and he could definitively say he knew that they couldn't have been in the woods, that left me with one thought.

Why didn't Mavis have her shotgun by the door?

She'd been gone when I showed up at her trailer. Where had she been? Then again, if she'd been out in the woods with her shotgun, shooting at me, why didn't she have it with her when she returned home?

"I don't know then," I said quietly. "Are you sure they were there the whole time?"

"I was requesitioning them for over an hour, Jacks," he replied. "And I picked them up at Bernie's right before. They looked like they'd been there for a good while, from the state of them."

I gave a resigned nod. What else could be said? If the Nelsons had been with Jeremy—and I knew he wouldn't lie for them, even with good reason—they weren't in the woods. If they weren't in the woods, they hadn't shot at me.

My brain went through the list of people who might know I'd go out to the woods. Or suspect that I was suspicious of Carter's death. One of them was sitting across from me. He had been at the police department with the other five suspects. None of the Nelsons had been available to be in the woods.

Of course, Jeremy could have been lying, but I knew that even if Jeremy had tried to shoot me in the woods, he wasn't dumb. He knew that I could easily find out if he had been lying about being at the police department with a single phone call. So, Jeremy and the Nelson were all off the list of suspects.

I'd seen Sawyer right before I'd gone out to the woods. He'd briefly mentioned the woods. Maybe he suspected that comment would send me out into the woods and he followed? Then there was Mavis. But even if she had been out in the woods shooting at me, she'd had no way to know I'd be out there. Or even suspect I'd be out there.

Unless she saw you walking the trail through her window.

That thought made me realize that anyone could have seen me walking through town towards the woods. *Anyone* could have seen me taking the trail. It started by Harper's. The possible list of suspects was infinite.

"Look," Jeremy sat forward, "why don't you get showered up?"

I sighed and took another gulp of steaming coffee, ignoring the burn once again.

"We'll get you in some clean clothes. Get you doctored up. And you can just stay here for the evening."

"I don't know."

"You'll feel safer. My bed is really comfortable," he said.

I looked up at him, a questioning eyebrow raised.

"I'd take the recliner for the night," Jeremy added quickly.

I might have been mistaken, but his cheeks flashed pink. After another gulp of hot coffee, I finally met his gaze.

"I have to get home to Rattlesnatches," I said. "I'll be just as safe at home."

Jeremy didn't argue, he simply gave me a slow nod.

"But," I said, "I'd be really happy if you'd take me."

He smiled.

"Want to borrow some slippers for the trip?" he asked.

"Please."

I pushed back to look under the table at my ravaged feet. They were never going to be the same.

"Do you want to go to the funeral with me tomorrow?" Jeremy asked as he rose from the table. "Pay your respects and all that?"

"I wouldn't miss it," I mumbled.

Chapter Twenty

Early evening darkness had encroached on the shop by the time I had settled back in at the check-out counter at the bookstore. A light drizzle was spattering the front windows of the bookstore and I'd turned on the space heater under the counter. My favorite cardigan was wrapped tightly around me as I tapped away at my laptop keyboard. Rattlesnatches was curled up in ball next to the cash register, snoring gently as he slumbered. Cozy as it was, I couldn't chase the chill from my bones.

After my foray into the woods and the chat with Jeremy at his house, all I could think about was how I'd barely escaped death. Having no solid proof of who had taken shots at me in the woods, paranoia creeped through every inch of my brain. While it was obvious that none of the Nelsons could have been behind the gunshots since they'd been with Jeremy at the time, everyone was a suspect in my book. Even my own mother would have drawn a suspicious gaze if I'd laid eyes on her at the moment.

Upon being delivered back to the shop by Jeremy, I'd spent over an hour in the bathroom cleaning up. Every square inch of my body was scrubbed clean. After my shower, I found that most of the scratches on my face and arms were superficial. They'd disappear in a few days. Fortunately, the bottoms of my feet proved to be in better shape than they'd felt.

Bruising from rocks and forest debris pushing against my soles was apparent, but they hadn't been hacked up. I applied medicine to the few scrapes, but not much was needed besides a thorough scrubbing. Putting on thick wool socks and my own slippers eased the pain as I walked downstairs to take up my post at the check-out counter again.

I hadn't bothered opening the shop for the remainder of the day.

My customers would simply have to deal with it.

For an hour, I did my best to straighten the shelves in the shop. Then I dusted the dark wood of the stairway banister and the shelves. Displays of books were straightened and sorted. After a quick organization of the check-out counter, my feet were angry with me, so I took up a post at my laptop. The rest of the evening would be spent in front of the space heater with my feet relaxed.

Head Rock Harbor Books had always been a safe space for me. Growing up in a chaotic household and having a childhood rife with instability, my aunt's store had always been a haven for me. It had always been one of the two places I could go to when my mom and dad were drinking and fighting. Which was often.

In the past, all through my childhood and early teen years, my mother and father had been infamous for their binge drinking and knock-down-drag-out fights. The Harper household had been a frequent visiting spot for the Head Rock Harbor police. Extra hands and feet would have to be grown for me to count how many times I saw the police handcuff one—or both—of my parents on the front lawn at the trailer.

Even after my father left, Deb and I stayed in the trailer park, and she continued drinking. It wasn't until my early teens, when I'd finally had enough and moved into the tiny apartment over the bookstore with my aunt, that Deb straightened up. It was nothing for her to lose a drunk husband who would beat on her. But when I gave up on Deb, she got into the program, straightened herself out, and worked on her future.

She'd been bequeathed the trailer park and restaurant by the former owner. A man she had taken up with after she got into the program. I didn't ask too many questions about her relationship with the elderly former owner of the properties. Specifics were not necessary. However, getting clean and having an affair had done wonders for my mother's financial situation.

The program, on the other hand, was hit or miss. My mother was sober ninety-nine percent of the time. However, the one percent where she slipped was rough. Though I still held a grudge, I had to give the woman credit for always scraping herself up and starting over. She didn't give up on her sobriety. And I always had my aunt and the bookstore to keep me safe when those slip ups inevitably came.

Even now, with my aunt gone and the store in my name, it was a refuge from the world.

But even it couldn't chase the chill from my bones.

I felt safe, but the memory of the woods would take more than a safe space to be forgotten. Shivers ran up my spine as the drizzle trickled down the windows at the front of the store. The droplets looked like molten gold in the light of the street lamps outside.

Tapping away at my laptop, my mind was scattered. Writing a single, comprehensible sentence was impossible. Frustrated, I closed my laptop and gave in to my worries. Without more rest, and a good sleep to clear my head, there was no way I could write. Even though I needed to attend Carter Nelson's funeral the following day, the shop was going to be closed for the next two days. I needed to forget my responsibilities and relax for two days for once.

I stood from the check-out counter and made my way around it, barely rousing Rattlesnatches from his slumber. He opened one eye to peek at me, then lazily shut it once again. Over at entrance, I stared out at the light misty rain falling outside. Puddles were beginning to form in the gutters of Harbor Street. The golden light from the street lamps made everything seem to glow.

With a sigh, I reached over and slapped the light switch next to the door. When I turned back to make certain the front door was locked up tight, a ghastly white face appeared in the window pane. Hollering in shock, I jumped back from the door. My eyes locked with Mavis Attberry's as she stared at me through the door, a look of panic on her face.

"*Jackson!*" her muffled voice came through the glass. "*Help me!*"

I started towards the door, then stopped myself. Mavis was staring at me with pleading eyes, but my mind flashed back to the woods. To her trailer. To the missing shotgun at her front door. Now she was standing outside my shop, where I was all alone, far after closing hours.

Shaking my head, I knew that I could trust Mavis. *I knew it.*

Quickly, I made my way back to the door and flipped the lock on the knob, then the deadbolt. As soon as I pulled the door in, the bells chiming overhead, Mavis pushed her way in out of the drizzle. Shaking her whole body like a dog, water droplets flew off of her raincoat in all directions. I shut the door behind her and locked it once again, unsure if I was making a wise decision to trap myself with her.

"What are you doing here, Mavis?" I asked, keeping space between us.

Just in case.

"Jackson," she turned to me, dropping her hood. "They done tried to get me!"

Mavis' short hair was sticking up in every direction. Between the wet of the weather and the static from her slick raincoat, her hair was a fright. Her glasses were already fogging over from the change in temperature and any bare flesh was dotted with rain.

"Who?" I asked, frowning.

"*Them!*" she demanded. "They were in my house!"

I held my hands up, trying to calm Mavis. She had to slow down and gather her thoughts so that I could make sense of what she had to say. Mavis harrumphed and wrapped her arms tightly around her middle as she stared at me.

"Who's trying to get you, Mavis?" I asked after a few moments. "What are you talking about?"

"Well, I—" Mavis started to rattle off her thoughts.

"Slowly," I said. "Take it slow."

Annoyed, but knowing I was right, Mavis took a breath. After collecting herself—and her thoughts—she looked me in the eyes.

"I was laid up in my recliner," she said as calmly as she could manage. "You know how I like to nap in front of the box?"

I nodded, remembering Mavis' penchant for starting her nightly sleep in front of the T.V. in her favorite chair. She'd always drift off watching an old murder mystery or detective show—maybe late-night trash T.V.—and then eventually move to her bed once she woke up to use the restroom.

"Okay," I said. "Yeah."

I glanced at the clock. It was only half past nine.

"Well, I woke up," Mavis said. "I was just about to get up and head into the bedroom. To do my nightlies, you know?"

I nodded again.

"And as soon as I got to my bedroom door, they came running out of my bedroom! Nearly knocked me on my keister!"

My eyes grew wide. "Who, Mavis? Who was in your bedroom?"

She opened her mouth, obviously to give the same pronouncement as before. However, she stopped herself suddenly and looked thoughtful.

"Well, I don't really know!" she cried. "They was wearing all black. Like one of them cat burglars! Nearly knocked me down gettin' out of my trailer!"

"Oh my gosh," I mumbled.

"Well, I got my shotgun from the closet—it took me a second to find it—because I was gonna blow a hole right where God already put one," Mavis growled. "But they was gone. My front door was just flappin' in the wind. All gone, Jackson!"

Mavis lurched forward and slumped against me. Automatically, I put my arms around her to keep her on her feet, but also to comfort her. For a few moments, I patted Mavis' back and held her, feeling less scared for my own safety now that I had someone else's safety to take up my concern. When it finally seemed like Mavis could hold herself together, I helped her stand up straight and put my hands on her shoulders.

"Mavis," I said, "you always keep your shotgun by the door. Why was it your closet?"

"Well, I—" Mavis began, but stopped herself once more.

"What?" I asked.

She frowned deeply.

"Well," she shook her head, "I don't know, Jackson. I must've left it there. When they ran down the hallway, I ran the other way. I was gonna hide in the closet—look for my baseball bat, but I saw the shotgun and grabbed it. I was going to—"

I waved her off.

"Got it," I said. "Mavis, you need to call Marv. Now."

"I ain't callin' that old—"

I stopped her. "If someone broke into your house, you need to have Marv check it out."

She glowered at me.

"He's not my favorite person, either," I said. "But the police need to take your statement and go check your trailer. They need to make sure it's safe. Okay?"

Mavis hemmed and hawed for a moment, but finally gave me a begrudging nod. I led her over to the check-out counter and nudged the phone at her. Moments later, she was talking up a storm to whoever had answered the non-emergent line at the police department.

Turning to look out at the night, a steadier rain was coming down now.

Why was Mavis' shotgun in her closet?

Chapter Twenty-One

Jeremy picked me up at the bookstore an hour before the funeral was to begin. He wasn't surprised to see Mavis with me. Both Jeremy and Marv had been to the bookstore the night before to take her statement. Such as it was. Then they'd gone to check out her trailer. After they had called the bookstore to let us know her trailer checked out as safe, Mavis had begged to stay the night. I'd set her up on my sofa and the two of us made it through a night of fitful sleep.

We dropped Mavis back at her trailer since she had no interest in attending the funeral, then Jeremy and I drove out to the highway. We got pizza from Casey's and sat in his car, discussing my near death in the woods, what had happened to Mavis, and Carter's strange death. Even with no one to interrupt us, no new theories came to mind. We were both at a loss as to why things were not adding up about Carter's death. Who had shot at me and broken into Mavis' house was another mystery that was no closer to being solved.

After the quick lunch of Casey's pizza, we made our way to Lankey's Funeral Home. Somehow, neither of us had gotten pizza sauce on our suits, so we didn't have to change before showing up at the funeral home. Which was fortunate since we were nearly running late. With only five minutes to spare, we lined up to get inside with everyone else.

Arliss Lankey, the owner of Lankey's Funeral Home, and head mortician, was shaking hands as everyone entered. However, due to the impending services, he was rushing the handshakes and ushering everyone inside quickly. He managed to give us both a warm hand and a genuine smile before Jeremy and I followed the throng of mourners into the chapel.

Due to our late arrival, Jeremy and I grabbed our programs from the usher at the entrance to the chapel and ducked inside quietly. As is common with small towns, everyone had shown up for Carter's funeral. Jeremy and I found two seats in a pew in the back row on the left side of the room and slid into them as discreetly as possible.

The heater at Lankey's was obviously in working order. Warmth from all of the bodies and the air from the vents was stifling. I made quick work with shrugging my peacoat off, letting it bunch up around me since there was no time to find a proper place to store it for the service. Jeremy followed my lead.

Carter Nelson was laid in his casket, dressed in a smart black suit. As was typical, the lower half of the casket was closed, but since his wounds were covered, the upper half of the casket was open. Sprays of roses were positioned at the head and foot of the casket. A large framed picture of him in happier times was on an easel near the foot of the casket. Behind him was the sanctuary and podium, where a preacher was making his way to speak.

A quick look around the funeral home as the doors were shut at the back let me know that I was not alone in being overwhelmed by the heat. Several mourners were using the programs to fan themselves. Others were using them to hide their mouths as they whispered to neighbors next to them in their pews. I could only guess at what rumors were being spread at such a somber event.

"That's his wife," Jeremy said, leaning closer to me. *"Carter's wife."*

I looked up as a woman sat down next to Myrna Carter and her sons in the front middle pew. Dressed in a smart and well-fitted, though somber, black pantsuit, the woman eased herself between Myrna and Colton Nelson. She wrapped an arm around Colton's shoulders, whose head was hung so low it could have been in his lap. The black cartwheel hat on her head was trimmed with a lilac ribbon and a sheer black veil.

That's a little much, even for a funeral. I thought.

"Where's she been all week?" I whispered back as the preacher began his sermon.

"She just got to town last night," Jeremy mumbled. *"Up from Burlington."*

I frowned.

"It's what? A two-hour drive? What took her so long to get here?"

Jeremy's shoulders rose and fell.

"She sure knows how to play the grieving widow," Jeremy mumbled out of the corner of his mouth.

I turned my head to look at him and we both grinned discreetly. Leave it to a best friend to know exactly what you had been thinking. Nudging him surreptitiously in the side, I turned my attention to the preacher and his sermon.

Straightening his back and sitting up, Jeremy followed my lead. We both had to be good Midwestern boys and behave at this event of respect and solemnity.

Over the years, I'd been to many funerals. When growing up in a small town, you tend to know everyone. Maybe everyone isn't your neighbor or best friend—and maybe you don't know everyone all that well—but you know of them. If someone in town dies, you either knew them or someone who loved them. Or both. Regardless of your affiliation with the actual deceased, you show up to the funeral as a show of support and respect.

One thing I knew for certain, Midwestern funerals were generally short and sweet; displays of hysterics were not tolerated. Big emotions were left for later in the day when the events were over and the aggrieved were left without an audience. After the funeral, there was sometimes a graveside service. If not, or after, everyone was hosted at the home of one of the family members of the deceased.

Dishes that were called "salads" that resembled anything but were eaten. Casseroles were demolished. The regular church people and other respectable folks drank soda pops. The relatives no one liked to mention drank beers. Everyone in town took time to eat, pay their condolences to the family, and bit by bit, everything came to an end.

If people were efficient about it, a funeral, graveside service, and the visit to the family home could be done in under two hours. One thing Midwesterners hated was wasting a weekend day mourning someone they may or may not have actually known all that well. Respect and support for the family was important, but no one wanted to get crazy about it.

My mind had wandered so far that I barely registered that the service was coming to a close. Jeremy had to bump me in the elbow to rise for the Benediction. Like the rest of the good church folks, I rose from the pew and listened to the preacher give the final words on the matter at hand. Then we all sat as music played—some old country song I didn't recognize, that must have been a favorite of Carter's—as the family filed out mournfully.

Mrs. Nelson and Colton were the first two down the aisle. Myrna followed directly behind, and then her boys brought up the tail. As they walked by the last pew, I caught Kenny's eye. He mumbled something to Hunter, and they both shot me a glare. I didn't return the look. I gave them a soft smile instead. Jeremy seemed to catch onto the look I got from the Nelson boys, and shifted angrily in his seat.

I laid a hand on his knee and gave it a squeeze.

I don't need anyone to fight my battles, I tried to say.

Jeremy relaxed, but he laid a hand over mine. Quickly, I slid my hand from under his. Jeremy didn't say anything, but he retracted his hand to his side and we both looked away from each other.

Finally, with the family out of the funeral home, it began to empty out. In efficient Midwestern fashion, the second row filed out next. Then the third, so on and so forth until only the back rows were left.

That was the Catch-22 about the back row. You could always find a seat when arriving late, but you were always the last to get to leave. With nowhere pressing to be, since neither of us planned to go to the graveside service or the family home, Jeremy and I stayed in our seats. We allowed everyone else to make their way out of the funeral home before we stood.

When it was two of us left and the line at the exit was shortening, the two of us finally stood. Jeremy wrapped an arm around my shoulder and gave me a squeeze, and I didn't pull away. However, I didn't lean into the hug much.

"Ready to go?" he asked quietly.

"I suppose," I said. "I have work waiting for me at the shop."

"I'm sure there's a game on I'm missing," Jeremy chuckled.

The two of us eased our way out of the pew towards the main aisle. As I was about to exit the row and turn into the aisle, a gasp from the front of the funeral home caught my attention. Jeremy and I both whipped around to see one of the ushers taking a tumble in front of the casket. I reached out, as though I could actually catch the man as a gasp escaped my throat.

Jeremy groaned as the man fell to the ground, the stack of leftover programs in his hands fluttering up around him, then floating to the ground like morbid confetti. Before either of us could rush to help him, the usher popped back up, brushing himself off. Jerking his head around to see who had seen his humiliation, his cheeks turned red when he saw us.

"You okay, Earl?" Jeremy asked. "That was quite a tumble."

"Yeah," the man replied. "Just a little clumsy, I 'spose."

Jeremy and I chuckled, hoping levity would lessen his embarrassment.

Poor guy, I thought as I watched him start picking up the slew of programs. Jeremy and I stepped into the aisle and headed towards the exit. Turning my head to check on the usher, I saw that he'd given up on picking up the programs and was trying to collect them into a pile by sweeping them with his feet as he walked around. Another usher rushed over and started to help. They were only managing to make a bigger mess of things.

My feet suddenly couldn't move. I was stuck in the aisle, my head turned to stare at the ushers. Jeremy stumbled to a stop. When he turned to check on me, I knew my mouth was hanging open and my eyes were glazed over with thought.

"Jacks?" Jeremy asked. "You okay?"

Blinking a few times, I felt the puzzle pieces falling into place.

"Mrs. Nelson!" I declared. "Is she still here?"

Jeremy shrugged. "Maybe? She's probably shaking hands out front?"

"Come on!" I said, rushing down the aisle, grabbing his elbow as I ran. "I have two questions for her."

Chapter Twenty-Two

"And you're *absolutely* certain?" I spoke hurriedly into the phone.

Head Rock Harbor Books was lit up, Rattlesnatches was sitting on his haunches in front of me at the check-out counter as I used the phone, and Jeremy was pacing. After I'd asked my questions of a confused Mrs. Nelson—she didn't know me from Adam—I hadn't explained myself to Jeremy. Instead, I'd grabbed his elbow again, thanking Mrs. Nelson as I ushered us back into Jeremy's car. During the five-minute drive back to the bookstore, I'd bounced in my seat, my mind whirling as Jeremy did his best to get me to talk.

I was unmoved. Until I made the one phone call that could help me put the last pieces of Carter Nelson's puzzle together, I'd keep my thoughts to myself. Even though Jeremy was my best friend, I couldn't risk sending a police officer off on a tear without a solid theory. Knowing Jeremy, one word from me, whether I was right or not, and he'd burn down the entire town. I couldn't be responsible for that happening.

Rapping my fingertips nervously against the wood check-out counter, I waited nervously for the response at the other end of the phone. Rattlesnatches batted softly at my fingers, thinking a game was being played. I reached up and scratched his head subconsciously as I held the phone to my ear.

"*Well,*" Bernie replied slowly, "*that's how I remember it. Yeah.*"

"And he's there now?" I asked.

"*Yeah.*"

"And she wasn't there then?" I asked.

"*Nope.*"

"Thanks, Bernie!" I smiled to myself. "Take care."

Bernie was giving a "goodbye" when I sat the phone back on its cradle. At the sound of the phone call ending, Jeremy stopped pacing and turned to me, expectant. I crossed my arms over my chest and stared at my friend.

"What?" he asked. "Who are we arresting?"

"You lied to me," I said.

Jeremy frowned deeply at me. After a pause, I realized I'd worded things wrong.

"Well, not a *lie*," I said. "An omission."

"What did I omit?" Jeremy grumbled.

"You didn't have all of the Nelsons with you yesterday in the interrogation room."

Jeremy looked around thoughtfully, then shrugged.

"What are you talking about?" he asked, then seemed to have a thought. "*The wife?* Are we going to arrest Mrs. Nelson?"

I didn't address that question.

"Myrna Nelson wasn't with you," I said. "You had the four boys. That's it."

Jeremy shrugged.

"Well, yeah. Why would I question Myrna? *Did she do it?*"

"You should have told me that, Germ!" I threw my hands up. "I might have figured this out a lot more quickly if you were a full disclosure kind of guy."

Jeremy, for what it's worth, didn't make an excuse. He simply mocked my gesture, throwing his hands dramatically in the air.

"How was I to know that was important?" he asked.

"*Everything* is important when you're solving a murder!"

"So…Carter was murdered? You're sure?"

I shook my head.

"Oh, good lord, Jacks," Jeremy slumped against the check-out counter. "Which is it? Suicide or murder? Because I can't take any more of this nonsense."

"Well, I—"

"Just tell me who to arrest," Jeremy pleaded with me. "Or if we need to just drop it."

"I—"

"Tell me what to do!" Jeremy demanded, but it came with a laugh.

He was exhausted. I understood that feeling. Putting him out of his misery was the biggest kindness I could do.

"You need to bring Colton Nelson to the P.D.," I said. "Put him in a cell. He's at Bernie's. Apparently, he wasn't into the whole graveside and family thing, either."

"Arrest Colton?" he nodded. "Got it."

"No," I said. "You need to pick him up and put him in a cell."

"I don't know what you're—"

"And Mavis Attberry," I said. "They both need to be in a cell. *Now.*"

Jeremy started to speak, his mouth opening and closing like a fish a few times. Finally, he shut his gob and gave me a firm nod.

"I'll do it," Jeremy said. "But only because you told me to."

"Good boy." I leaned across the counter and tousled his golden curls.

He pretended to be offended, but I caught the ghost of a grin at the corner of his mouth.

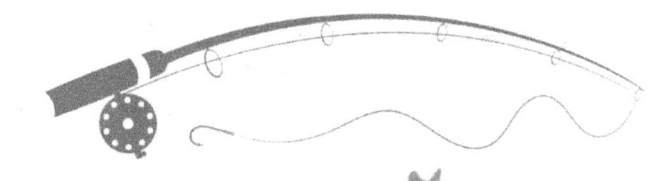

Chapter Twenty-Three

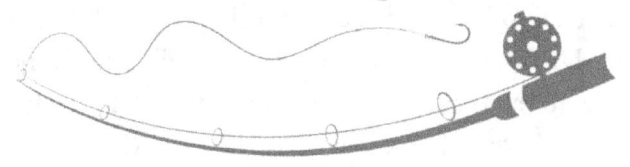

Marv wasn't exactly happy with being left out of the decision-making process Jeremy and I had gone through at my shop. He was glowering in our direction as the three of us sat in the front room of the police department. I'd asked him to trust me while we waited for the fireworks. Begrudgingly, he was leaning against the desk currently occupied by Officer Riley, half-sitting, with his arms laced firmly across his chest. Jeremy was mirroring Marv's position on the desk opposite Officer Riley's, and I was seated in the chair behind it, mirroring Officer Riley.

Until the inevitable happened, the three of us were going to have a staring contest with a dollop of the silent treatment. Officer Ashley Riley was doing his best to pretend that he was the only person in the room. He kept his head down, looking at his desk, working on the file that currently needed an updated report.

Getting Mavis out of her trailer and into a cell had taken some doing. Fortunately, with me by his side, Jeremy had less trouble than he would have had if he had shown up to her house with Marv or Riley. I was able to cajole Mavis into the police car and into a cell without any violence. Colton Nelson, on the other hand, came with us as if he had been expecting us.

We'd gone to Bernie's, and when Jeremy sidled up behind him at the bar and laid a hand on his shoulder, Colton simply looked up, nodded, and followed us out. He'd gotten into the back of the police car and ridden with us in silence to the P.D. When Jeremy led him to a cell, he said nothing and let Jeremy lock him up without incident. Barely thirty minutes had passed since we'd picked up Mavis. Only ten since Colton had been placed in his cell.

Any minute now, I thought to myself as I stared at Marv.

A glaze settled over my eyes as I stared at the police chief. Mentally, I was going over the data I'd collected. Though I was certain I was right, the little voice in my head kept giving me the *what if* scenario that I couldn't quite shake. I'd asked Jeremy to put his rear on the line by picking up Mavis and Colton. If I was wrong, Marv was going to throw me in a cell.

He'd possibly take Jeremy's badge, too. Or bump him from Detective back down to Officer. From the look on his face, Jeremy and I could potentially end up cellmates if I was wrong. Fortunately, I didn't have to wait long to find out how things would play out. As expected, the lobby door of the police department burst open and all the expected players spilled through.

Kenny, Mason, Hunter, and Myrna fought to be the first through the door. Once the jam was cleared, with Myrna somehow winning the shoving match, the three boys stumbled into the lobby. Mrs. Nelson, looking traumatized, shuffled in behind them, worry etched across her face.

The lobby erupted into a chorus of demands and condemnations as Mrs. Nelson stood there, confused by the ruckus. Jeremy stayed leaning against the desk as I sat there watching. Officer Riley tucked his head into his report as Marv held his hands up, doing his best to silence the Nelson family.

"You all just settle down!" Marv demanded. "I won't let you turn my department into a three-ring circus!"

The Nelsons were not to be settled.

"You get Colton out of that cell right now, Marvin Bucksworth!" Myrna demanded with a witchy-poo finger jabbed at his face. "He is innocent! This is a travesty!"

"He didn't do anything!" Kenny bellowed, backing up his mother. "Mavis Attberry is who you're after!"

"Yeah!" Hunter and Mason echoed. "Mavis did it!"

It was clear that Marv had tolerated enough in the few seconds he'd allow them to scream. He pulled his gun from his holster, and though he didn't point it at anyone in particular, his intention was clear.

The action seemed unwarranted and an escalation that was not quite needed to me. However, I wasn't police chief. What Marv chose to do was his business. One way or another, he would get peace and order in his police department.

The Nelsons fell quiet immediately, though they didn't stop glaring murderously at the chief. I'd never really felt worried for Marv's life before, but from the looks on the four faces before him, I was certain if he hadn't had a gun, he'd have had a big problem.

"You four just settle your hash right now," Marv said. "Or you'll all be in cells, too!"

Myrna opened her mouth to speak. Before she could get a word out, I broke in calmly.

"Mavis did what?" I asked.

Myrna's mouth shut and all five Nelsons—Mrs. included—turned to look at me. Marv kept his gun out, but turned his head to look at me as well. Jeremy sat up straight on the desk, making it clear that anyone who came for me would have to go through him. When none of the Nelsons answered me, I stood slowly from my seat.

"What did Mavis do, Hunter? Mason? Why do you think Marv needs to arrest Mavis, Kenny?" I asked.

All three boys glared at me. Myrna scowled.

"I was under the impression you all thought Carter committed suicide?" I asked, keeping Jeremy and the desk between me and the four of them. "So…what do you think Mavis should be arrested for?"

"She's already in a cell, anyway!" Marv barked at them.

"Good!" Myrna crowed. "She did it. Not Colton!"

"Again," I asked calmly, silencing everyone, "what did she do?"

Myrna glared at me. She knew she couldn't answer that. All three boys exchanged glances, their cheeks red.

"Anyone gonna answer him?" Marv demanded.

"We don't have to answer anything!" Myrna jabbed her hands into her hips. "You get Colton out of that cell right now."

"They don't have to answer me, Marv," I said, stopping him before he could wave his gun around some more. "But, if you don't mind, have them sit down to listen to me for a few minutes."

"We don't have to—" Kenny growled.

Marv was waving his gun again.

"All four of you sit down!" Marv barked, brandishing his gun menacingly once more. "Get in them chairs right now or you're all going into a cell! Meats in the seats now!"

Mrs. Nelson's face was ghostly white, and though she wasn't one of the four Marv was referring to, she quickly took a seat in one of the chairs lined along the front wall of the lobby. When Myrna, Kenny, Hunter, and Mason realized Marv wasn't simply threatening them, they begrudgingly stomped over to the seats. One by one, they all flopped into the chairs, scowling at the three police officers and me.

I gave them a moment, then rounded the desk, though I didn't get any closer to them than necessary. Marv and Jeremy had to have time to jump between us if things went awry.

"So," I said, "one thing I know for certain. Carter Nelson is dead."

"No crap, ya' genius!" Kenny started to stand.

Marv lurched forward and Kenny fell back into his seat.

"You all stay in your seats until you've been excused," Jeremy said calmly. "This will be your last warning."

The scowls and red faces didn't disappear, but it was clear that the understanding was final.

"Carter is dead," I said. "You have my deepest sympathies. All of you."

I chewed at my lip for a moment.

"But here's the thing," I began. "When Mavis was arrested for taking his watch from the trail the other day, you dropped charges against her because *you didn't want an innocent woman in jail.* She was innocent then in your eyes. What made you change your mind?"

Slowly, the redness drained from the Nelsons' faces. Their eyes darted back and forth as they exchanged glances.

"I think you want her to be guilty now…because you think Colton is guilty. And he's in a cell. So, instead of him taking the blame for what happened to Carter, you'd rather pin it on Mavis. Even if you know she's innocent. Better her than your own, right?"

None of the Nelsons responded.

"When Colton wasn't under suspicion, it was safe to say Mavis was innocent. You didn't want her punished for something you know she didn't do—especially since everyone believed Carter had committed suicide. No one was suspected of his murder at the time. You were all essentially free and clear. So why blame Mavis when suicide could be the cause of death, right?"

Again, no responses from the Nelsons.

"Here's the other thing," I said. "Mavis didn't do it. You all know it. I know it. Mavis knows it. She's in a cell right now for protection. In case any of you decided to stop by her trailer before coming here."

"Why would we—" Myrna began.

"Because two of you were there yesterday," I said, cutting her off. "Isn't that right?"

Again, more nervous shifting and glances from the Nelsons.

"So," I began to pace back and forth in front of the Nelsons, "Carter is dead. And three of you helped move his body."

"I won't listen to this!" Kenny demanded and started to rise.

"You better marry that hind end to that plastic, son," Marv growled.

Kenny slumped back into his seat. I waited to make sure the Nelsons were staying orderly, then began again.

"Let's start at the beginning," I said.

I swept a hand at the Nelson boys.

"The three of you met Carter and Colton out at their campsite. Did some fishing probably. Caught up on old times. Those kinds of things. As dark started to fall, you all invited Carter and Colton up to Harper's. Unconcerned with what he was about to lead his son to, Carter agreed. Colton was more than willing to join in on the festivities."

The boys exchanged glances. Myrna stared down at her lap.

"The five of you walked the trail up towards Harper's," I said. "As you got close—I'd say up around Wilford Road—Carter realized that this was not good clean fun. The three of you were taking them to a bar. Inevitably, his son—who has a drinking problem—would be tempted to drink. Mrs. Nelson, you told me outside the church earlier today that Colton has been in the program for a while, right?"

"Well, yes," Mrs. Nelson responded sheepishly. "It was rather rude of you, honestly."

"I'm sorry for asking such a personal question at the time," I said. "It was unfortunate, but there wasn't time to wait for a better time. And I hope you now realize that my intention behind the question was to seek justice for your husband."

She said nothing, but sat back in her seat.

"So," I continued, "Carter became enraged that his three nephews were so insensitive as to take their cousin to a bar when they knew he was an alcoholic. He was *infuriated* that his son was giving up on his sobriety."

"We weren't—" Mason began.

Marv shushed him with a wave of his gun.

"Carter and Colton got into a fight on the trail," I said, ignoring Mason. "It got heated. The three of you left them there to fight out their father and son troubles. That about right?"

I waited for the three boys to exchange glances once again. Finally, Kenny nodded for the group.

"Thought so," I said. "Then Colton joined the three of you at Harper's. Carter wasn't with him. He told you Carter was going back to the campsite. Or that Carter wasn't coming. It doesn't really matter. That check out, too?"

Kenny nodded again without conferring with the others.

"So," I said, "the four of you got to drinking, having a good time, dancing, flirting with the ladies, but after a few hours you all got concerned about Carter. I'm guessing that you, Kenny, went to check on Carter first. You seem like the leader here."

Kenny glowered at me.

"You're the reason for the button on the trail near Wilford Road," I said. "Dragging a body can leave behind all kinds of evidence."

Enraged, Kenny's face flamed, but he said nothing.

"Kenny killed Carter?" Jeremy asked in shock.

I ignored the question.

"You took him to the trail head and rolled him down the hill," I said. "Disposed of the evidence. Then you went back and told everyone he was fine."

Mason and Hunter were shifting uncomfortably in their seats.

"Now, I'm not sure which of you went next to check on Carter," I said, "but whoever it was found Carter's dead body. To cover up what you thought Kenny did—since he'd said Carter was fine—you moved the body further down the trail towards the campsite. Then you went back and told everyone Carter was fine. Kenny was probably shocked at the time, but whatever."

Hunter was looking anywhere but at me, so I had a pretty good idea who had been the second brother to move Carter's body.

"Finally," I said, as the night wore on, "*Mason* went to check on Carter, found his body on the trail, dragged it back to the campsite, put a shotgun to his chest as the body laid there, and fired off one round. Probably wiped the gun clean and then put Carter's hands on it to leave prints. Trying to cover up for your brothers. Am I right?"

Mason didn't answer. He mimicked Hunter's behavior. Only Kenny and Myrna had the nerve to stare up at me.

"Are you saying that—" Marv began, but I cut him off, too.

"So, things just got out of control for y'all," I said. "Next thing you know, Mavis has Carter's watch and is pawning it. You couldn't let an innocent woman rot for what you did, so you dropped charges and pushed the suicide narrative. You all would have felt too guilty—*at the time*—if you let Mavis swing for something you *knew* she hadn't done."

Two glares and two hung heads met me once again. Mrs. Nelson looked absolutely scandalized. She turned her head to stare at her family.

"Things got hairy, though," I said. "That's mostly my fault. Kenny realized that I was spending time collecting evidence, talking to Colton, and you all had to do something to take suspicion off Colton once again."

"What did they do?" Jeremy asked, breathlessly.

"Officer Riley," I asked, "would you go find out from Mavis if Myrna stopped by to…*buy some tomatoes* from her yesterday?"

Before Officer Riley could rise from his seat, Myrna was answering for Mavis.

"So what?" Myrna barked. "Everyone does it! It's no big deal!"

"It's illegal," Marv said gruffly.

"Well, you don't ever do anything to Mavis, so you can't do anything to me!" Myrna smirked.

"That's not how the law works, Myrna," I shook my head and chuckled. "Regardless, you went to Mavis' yesterday to…purchase some happiness, shall we say?"

Myrna didn't respond. I didn't expect her to answer me.

"You saw me walking the trail towards the woods when you were on her front porch," I said. "You knew I was going to look for more evidence. And when she had her back turned, you grabbed her shotgun from its spot by her front door. Then you followed me to the woods and fired a few rounds at me. I don't actually think you intended to harm me in any way. Just spook me. And make me think that if someone *had* murdered Carter, it wasn't Colton. It was Mavis."

"She has her shotgun!" Kenny barked. "How did my momma do that if Mavis has her shotgun?"

I grinned at him.

"It's funny you bring that up," I said. "Only the person that broke into her house last night and returned it would be certain she had it. Now I know which one of you did that. Also, you could have simply put her shotgun by the front door—*where she always keeps it*—and she never would have known you poked your head inside since she was asleep in her recliner."

Kenny sputtered as his face turned red as a tomato, and he sunk into his seat.

"So, dead body," I said. "Three people moving it. One shooting it. A mother trying to protect her nephew and sons."

"So, who killed him?" Jeremy pleaded with me.

"Really, Jackson," Marv backed him up. "And why?"

"Kenny," Officer Riley spoke up for once. "He was the first to go check on Carter."

"Oh," Marv and Jeremy answered simultaneously.

"I didn't kill him!" Kenny said. "You can't prove anything!"

He crossed his arms over his chest and sat up defiantly straight.

"Kenny Nelson," Marv began, "I'm placing you under—"

"I believe you, Kenny," I said, holding an arm out to stop Marv. "Because Carter was already dead when you found him on the trail. You were just the first to move the body."

"*What?*" Jeremy gasped.

"Carter was dead when Kenny found him," I repeated. "You moved the body to protect Colton. Didn't you?"

Kenny wouldn't meet my eyes, and he wouldn't answer me. Obviously, he didn't want to go to jail for murder, but he didn't want to throw his cousin under the bus, either.

"So, Colton did it?" Marv asked quickly.

Looking up and down the row of Nelsons, I couldn't help but feel bad for all of them. They were reckless, stupid, and a bit dangerous, but I still felt poorly.

"No," I said. "Colton didn't do it."

All eyes moved to Mrs. Nelson.

"And it wasn't Mrs. Nelson," I stopped their speculation quickly. "She truly just got into town last night."

Her eyes bugged that there would even be such a suggestion.

"Then just tell us, Jacks," Jeremy said. "Please."

I shrugged.

"No one killed Carter Nelson," I said.

Every set of eyes in the room widened and turned to me.

"The other question I asked you at the funeral, Mrs. Nelson?" I asked. "Whether or not your husband had high blood pressure?"

Nodding slowly, Mrs. Nelson stared at me.

"Has for years. But he refuses to do anything about it. Refuses to go back to the doctor more than he has to," she said, then looked thoughtful. "*Refused.*"

Tears started to stream down her face. I didn't want to continue, but I knew that everything had to be settled. If not for Carter's sake, then for his wife's and son's.

"Carter Nelson died of an aortic dissection," I said. "From too many years of unregulated high blood pressure. Probably triggered by the heated argument with Colton on the trail. I'm betting he started to march away when Colton left him on the trail to go to Harper's, but he didn't make it far. The aortic dissection was mentioned in his autopsy report, but the medical examiner assumed it was bisected from the shotgun blast to the chest. When I read it, I assumed the same. However, when Kenny found his body, he assumed Colton had killed his father. So…he tried to hide the body for the time being. Then Hunter did the same, essentially. Finally, we had Mason with the coup de grâce."

Everyone was stunned.

"Carter died of natural causes. You boneheads just made it look like a murder. If you'd simply called 911 when you found his body," I glared at Kenny, "we'd have known that a week ago. And you never would have had to worry about Colton being suspected of anything. Instead, you dragged his body all over God's creation, dropping buttons and pieces of clothing, and his watch. You did the one thing you didn't want done. You made his death look suspicious."

Jeremy had to stifle a laugh. I shot him a look and he did his best to look somber. Marv grumbled a warning at him, though I could tell he wanted to laugh as well.

"Now's the time to deny it if you want to," I said. "And Marv can arrest someone for murder instead. Probably Colton since he was the last to see his father alive."

Mrs. Nelson gasped. The Nelson boys and Myrna all exchanged glances. Mrs. Nelson was glaring angrily at all of them. Finally, Myrna, turned to look at me.

"That's about right, I suppose," she said.

Marv and Jeremy let out audible breaths behind me. My expression didn't change.

"I asked Jeremy to pick up Mavis to protect her. I had him pick up Colton for the same reason. I didn't know what wild thing the four of you might come up with if you knew that we were coming for y'all. You've already ruined his life enough," I admonished them calmly.

The boys and Myrna had the good sense to look ashamed. Mrs. Nelson was enraged with her husband's family.

"But," Mason squeaked, "that means we're all off the hook, right? Colton can be let go and the rest of us can go home. Right?"

I let Marv answer that question.

"Desecrating a corpse. Destruction of and tampering with evidence. False police reports. Lying to police officers. Purchasing illegal substances. Breaking and entering. Firing a shotgun at Jackson?" He started listing off their offenses. "Intimidating witnesses? Colton can go for sure. As can his mother. The rest of you numbskulls are in deep—"

"Marv," I shook my head at him.

"Well," he straightened himself, "you're all in trouble. If that answers your question."

I sighed. Carter Nelson had died. Naturally. That was good. In a way. But he had not seen an ounce of respect since his death. I was exhausted.

"Jeremy," I asked, "can I get Mavis and take her home now? I'm tired."

"Sure, Jacks," he answered softly. "I'll go get her and I'll take the two of you home."

"We'll walk," I said, turning to look at the Nelsons. "I think Marv is going to need your help more than we will."

Chapter Twenty-Four

The sun was barely starting to come up over the horizon when I left the bookstore on foot the following morning. Even though it was a Monday, it was still early, so the streets were quiet. With the new bookstore hours, I was going to enjoy my second day off. Sunday had essentially been taken from me—solving a murder will do that—and I was determined to have one good day in my first two-day weekend in a long time. However, I had one bit of business to tend to before I could relax for the rest of the day.

As I walked south from the bookstore towards Harper's, it crossed my mind that I'd likely have emails in my inbox from my agent, editor, and publisher. They'd all be wanting an update on where I was with the sixth book in the *Detective Randy Melton Mystery series*. Though I knew it wasn't exactly professional to keep them waiting, one more day wouldn't hurt them. I'd written five best sellers for them already. They could give me twenty-four hours of peace.

An Artful Assault, the working title of the sixth Harrison Garner, was shaping up nicely. Now, with my head free of worry about Carter Nelson's death, I had time to devote to writing. I could already tell that with my clear head I could easily bang out the last few chapters in the next few weeks. I'd ship the first draft off to the powers that be, wait for my notes, and start the next step in the publishing process.

Redrafting and editing.

Shaking as a tingle tickled up my spine, I couldn't help but laugh. Writing a story is one thing. Rewriting it seventy-seven more times is another. By the time I'd finished each book, I was thoroughly tired of it. If I never read one of my books again, I wouldn't be upset. Knowing that other people got enjoyment out of them made it all worthwhile, though.

Harper's Bar, Grill, Bait & Tackle was quiet as a churchyard when I arrived. The lights were off inside, the neon wasn't flickering, and the parking lot was empty. The sodium lights were still buzzing, though they were slowly dimming as the sun rose. I didn't stop at Harper's. My mother's restaurant wasn't my intended destination.

I continued on around the building into the trailer park. Making my way quietly along the dirt road that wound its way through the park, I did my best to be discreet. When I finally got to Mavis' trailer, I stood behind one of the bushes, watching her trailer for a moment. I wanted to make sure that all the lights were out and no movement could be detected. Mavis was never awake so early, but one could never be too careful.

When I was certain that she had not risen early for this particular day, I deftly, yet quietly, tiptoed my way across her yard. Up the deck stairs I crept, across the porch, and to her door. No sound could be heard through the thin front door of the trailer, so I reached into my back pocket and extracted the reason for my visit. Swiftly, I transferred the folded envelope from my back pocket through the mail slot in the side of Mavis' trailer. I eased the flap of the slot down gently, making as little noise as possible.

The gentle "tick" sound of the flap closing made me cringe, though I knew it only sounded loud to me since I was trying so hard to be quiet. Without another thought, I turned on my heels, intending to dash back across the porch and down the deck stairs. However, when I turned, I froze at the sight across the yard.

Jeremy's car was sitting on the dirt road at the end of the path leading up to Mavis' trailer.

I hadn't even heard his car approaching. I wanted to reach up and slap myself in the head for being so distracted that I hadn't heard him, but nothing could be done. Our eyes met across the yard and he waved me over. Sighing, I left the porch quietly and tiptoed across Mavis' yard to the driver's window of Jeremy's car.

"Get in, Jacks," Jeremy said quietly.

With no other option, I crept around to the passenger side, popped the door as quietly as possible, and slid into the passenger seat. Closing the door without making any noise was difficult, but I did my best. Once I had my seatbelt on, Jeremy let his foot off the brake, his car creeping down the dirt road away from Mavis' trailer. Once we got closer to Harper's, he applied more pressure to the gas.

We drove back across town in under a minute—Head Rock Harbor's downtown is miniscule, after all—and we were soon parked in front of the bookstore. I undid my seatbelt, but I made no move to get out of the car. Jeremy put it into park and turned it off, undoing his seatbelt immediately after. When he turned in his seat and kicked a knee up to look at me, I sighed.

"What was that about?" he asked.

"What was what about?"

"Why were you at Mavis Attberry's house?" he asked again.

"Just dropping something of hers off," I replied.

Jeremy nodded slowly. His head turned to look out the windshield for a brief moment as he sucked at his teeth.

"I always wondered how she paid the lot rent to your mom every month," Jeremy said. "Never really concerned myself with it too much since it wasn't a problem—but I was always curious."

I continued to stare straight ahead.

"Figured she was selling lots of...*tomatoes*," Jeremy whispered the final word playfully. "But I can be a good detective too sometimes."

A smile formed on my lips whether I wanted it to or not.

"How long have you been giving her money?" Jeremy asked.

"I haven't been giving Mavis money," I said simply.

Jeremy frowned at me.

"At least," I said, "as far as Mavis is concerned. I wouldn't take away her dignity like that."

"Ah," Jeremy said. "Does she think the Rent Fairy is pushing an envelope of money through her mail slot each month?"

I shrugged. "I don't care what she tells herself."

Jeremy stared at the side of my head as I stared through the windshield, seeing nothing.

"I've always wondered why you live so frugally," Jeremy said quietly. "I guess now I know. You don't have money to do much because you're giving it to that old—"

"I'll never be able to give her enough," I said. "Not without her knowing. Six hundred and fifty bucks a month is nothing compared to what I owe her."

"How can you owe that cranky old—"

"You know," I said, cutting him off again, "when my mom and dad would drink themselves stupid and beat on each other, I had Mavis. I could always run over to her trailer when things got really bad. She'd make me a peanut butter and jelly sandwich, give me some juice, and make the sofa up for me. Even in the dead of night, if I banged on her trailer door, she let me in and took care of me, Germ."

Jeremy had thoroughly shut his mouth.

"She's not the monster this town makes her out to be," I continued, staring straight ahead. "If it wasn't for her—and my aunt—I don't know what I would have done. And she never asked anything for it. She's never asked me for one thing in my entire life. She never asks *anyone* for anything."

A sigh came from Jeremy, but it wasn't derision.

"So what if she sells her *tomatoes*," I said, shrugging. "She's sassy and loud and obnoxious and a drunk. Sometimes she'll get a little funny with her shotgun. She's harmless. She couldn't hurt a fly if she wanted to. Not even if you paid her. Because under all of it, there's a woman who would take in a kid from a dangerous situation in the middle of the night, feed him, and give him a safe place to lay his head for a few hours so he could get sleep for school the next day."

Silence came from Jeremy's side of the car, but he was still turned, watching me.

"Everyone in this town can think what they want of Mavis," I said, "but that's the Mavis I know. Paying her lot rent each month so she can keep her home and her dignity is nothing. It's the bare minimum."

"Your mom wouldn't kick her out."

"No," I said, "but then mom would have to explain to the other renters why Mavis gets a pass and they don't. And Mavis wouldn't have it."

"But you need that money," Jeremy said, though his words were gentle. "The bookstore can't be making *that* much. And you can't do without to support her."

Desperately, I wanted to tell Jeremy that I had more money than I knew what to do with for the rest of my life. I wanted to tell him that I lived simply because I'd always lived simply. It had been how I grew up. It was what I knew. Money was security to me, nothing else.

"I have enough," I said. "My bills are paid. I get plenty to eat."

I patted my stomach, though there wasn't much there. Jeremy chuckled.

"I'm warm. Rattlesnatches eats like a king," I added. "I need for nothing, Germ."

He sighed again.

"All right," he said.

We sat there in silence for a few more moments, me staring out at Harbor Street, him staring at me.

"Can I ask you one question?"

"Sure."

I hoped his question wouldn't be about my financial situation. The truth was so close to spilling from my mouth, and I wasn't quite ready to trust anyone with my biggest secret.

"How'd you finally figure out what had happened to Carter?" he asked.

I relaxed.

"The ushers at the funeral," I said.

"The ushers?"

"The one who dropped the programs and the other one that tried to help him pick them up?"

"How'd that help you?" he asked.

"Earl dropped the programs," I reminded him. "They made such a mess. Scattered everywhere. And he was trying to pick them up, but got tired of it. He started trying to kick them into the pile. The other usher joined in, and…it made me realize that sometimes when a person tries to fix a problem the easy way, it just makes a bigger mess."

Jeremy snorted.

"It was simply the thing that made all the puzzle pieces fit," I shrugged. "The buttons and ripped cloth in weird places. The livor mortis. The abrasions in weird places. The Nelsons dropping charges on Mavis. Getting shot at in the woods. All of it made no sense. I couldn't figure out how one person could be responsible for everything. *It was one big mess.* Then I realized that the mess had gotten bigger as the week went by. *Obviously,* I had been looking at things wrong. The mess got so big because so many people were involved."

"Big messes," Jeremy chuckled. "I know a thing or two about that."

I smiled.

"Anyway," I said, "it made things click into place. It's crazy, but that was it."

"Crazy solved a mur—a case?" Jeremy questioned. "I don't even know what to call this one."

"Unfortunate," I said simply.

"I don't know what he'll get to stick," Jeremy informed me, "but Marv is planning to throw the book at the Nelsons."

"What about Colton?" I asked.

"His mom took him back to Burlington last night," Jeremy said. "I gave her some information about treatment programs for him."

"I hope he gets help."

Jeremy looked at me for a moment longer, then nodded. He turned slowly in his seat, his knee falling so that his feet were back in the floorboard on his side of the car. Silence overtook the car, and we both stared out at Harbor Street together.

"You're off work today," Jeremy said suddenly. "New hours at the bookstore and all."

"Yeah."

"I have the day off," he added. "Marv decided I've earned a little R and R."

"That was nice of him."

"It was," Jeremy said. "Since we're both off, and we both deserve some rest, do you…would you want to come over?"

I said nothing.

"Come hang out at my place for the day?" Jeremy asked.

The question was presented gently, yet so directly, there was no mistaking the implication of what Jeremy was asking of me. For a moment, I had no idea what to say. Jeremy and

I had been best friends since we were kids. No answer seemed right. Finally, I stopped staring out at Harbor Street and turned my head to look at him. He deserved to be looked in the eyes.

"I'm going to have to think about that," I answered.

Jeremy stared into my eyes, saying nothing.

"If that's okay?" I asked.

He nodded.

"Sure, Jacks," he said. "Whatever you need."

"Good work, though?" I held my hand out.

"Every Sherlock has to have his Watson," Jeremy said, turning in his seat again to shake my hand.

"Every Kiyoshi Mitari has to have his Kazumi Ishioka," I agreed.

"Every Velma has the rest of the Scoobies."

"Every Joe Friday has his Bill Gannon."

"Every Nancy has to have her Bess or George."

"Every Morse has to have his Lewis." I sassed.

"Every Green Hornet has to have his Kato." Jeremy shook his face in mine.

"Every Jessica Fletcher has to have her Dr. Seth Hazlitt," I added.

"Poirot has his Hastings," Jeremy grumbled.

"Brown has his Flambeau," I said.

"*Michael Knight has his KITT!*"

"*Every—*"

Jeremy's hands were suddenly on either side of my face and his lips were on mine. Shocked by the sudden development, I nearly pulled away. Instinct told me to pull way. Because I was supposed to be offended. Jeremy hadn't asked if he could kiss me. He'd given no indication that it was even on his mind. I was going to push him away and call him any number of names.

But the kiss was so good.

I didn't reach out and grab Jeremy like he'd grabbed me, but I found my eyes closing as my body fell into the kiss naturally. For what seemed like an eternity but not long enough—since that's how all great kisses work—Jeremy kissed me right there in the front seat of his car, parked outside of my shop. When he finally pulled away, it took a moment for me to pry my eyes open. But when I did, his hands had slid down to either side of my neck, caressing the flesh there gently as we stared at each other.

I didn't speak for a moment, afraid of how my voice would sound, but I finally found my words.

"I'm going to have to think about that," I said. "If that's okay?"

"Sure, Jacks. Whatever you need." Jeremy's voice was thick as pancake syrup.

I needed to have breakfast.

He smiled, though it didn't reach his eyes. Without another word, I pulled away and popped the car door open and slid out. I leaned down to give him a simple "thanks," and closed the door. Watching as Jeremy started the car and drove off quietly down Harbor Street, I couldn't help but wonder if I'd given him the right answer. Something inside of me told me that time was needed to know for sure, though. A kiss, years in the making, doesn't need an immediate decision.

Finally, once Jeremy had turned the corner and his car crept out of sight, I turned around to the bookstore. Rattlesnatches was standing up on his hind legs, his front legs on the windowsill, and he was staring out at me. I couldn't help but smile when I saw him there, waiting on me.

"You're so nosy," I said. "Mind your business."

Rattlesnatches' little mouth opened and closed, and though I couldn't hear him through the glass, I knew his response. It would have sounded like a *meow* to anyone else, but I knew he'd said, "*you are my business.*" I let myself into the bookstore, locking the door securely behind me. I'd played detective enough as Jackson Harper. It was time to put on Harrison Garner's hat for the rest of my day off.

PRIDE AND PUNCTURE (HEAD ROCK HARBOR MYSTERY #3) – coming to you in early 2025!

About the Author

Chase Connor spends his days writing about the people who live (loudly and rent-free) in his head when he's not busy being enthusiastic about naps and Pad Thai. Chase started his writing career as a confused gay teen looking for an escape from reality. Ten years later, one of the books he wrote during those years, *Just A Dumb Surfer Dude: A Gay Coming-of-Age Tale*, was published independently. Chase has numerous projects in various stages of completion lined up for publishing. Chase is a multi-genre author, but always with a healthy dollop of gay.

Chase can be reached at
chaseconnor@chaseconnor.com
Or on Twitter @ChaseConnor7
On Bluesky as chaseconnorbooks
He can also be found on his website www.chaseconnor.com.
or on Goodreads

SIGN UP FOR THE CHASE CONNOR BOOKS NEWSLETTER AT CHASECONNOR.COM

Chase has several novellas/novels for sale in e-book, paperback, hardback, and audiobook formats wherever books are sold.

www.ingramcontent.com/pod-product-compliance
Lightning Source LLC
Chambersburg PA
CBHW071853220626
47052CB00002B/93